PRAISE FOR *MYRRH*

"Clever, insightful, and insidiously vicious, Polly Hall's *Myrrh* is a terrifying and profoundly visceral exploration of social appearances, identity, and family. One of the most remarkable novels I've read in quite some time."
Eric LaRocca, author of *Things Have Gotten Worse Since We Last Spoke*

§

"*Myrrh* swirls with sharp prose and personality. A dynamite stick of a book, pregnant with pathos and nitroglycerin."
Hailey Piper, Bram Stoker® Finalist, and author of *A Light Most Hateful*

§

"Nothing can quite prepare you for the gift that is *Myrrh*, which mischievously reads like an unhinged Rumplestiltskin, a Daphne du Maurier suckerpunch, a Catriona Ward whirlpool of vertiginous proportions. Remember the name Polly Hall. Her novel breathes life in the gathering gloom."
Clay McLeod Chapman, author of *What Kind of Mother* and *Ghost Eaters*

§

"A festering account of the horrors women hold within their wombs, and the ones their daughters inherit."
Lindy Ryan, author of *Bless Your Heart* and *Cold Snap*

MYRRH

POLLY HALL

TITAN BOOKS

Myrrh
Hardback edition ISBN: 9781789095357
E-book edition ISBN: 9781803364971

Published by Titan Books
A division of Titan Publishing Group Ltd
144 Southwark Street, London SE1 0UP
www.titanbooks.com

First edition: April 2024
10 9 8 7 6 5 4 3 2 1

This is a work of fiction. All of the characters, organisations,
and events portrayed in this novel are either products of the
author's imagination or are used fictitiously. Any resemblance
to actual persons, living or dead (except for satirical
purposes), is entirely coincidental.

A CIP catalogue record for this title is available
from the British Library.

Printed and bound by CPI (UK) Ltd, Croydon, CR0 4YY.

For my family

Myrrh

from Arabic 'bitter'

*Myrrh is harvested by repeatedly wounding the tree
to make it bleed tears of aromatic gum.*

Maybe I was just born bad. But I was only taking what was rightfully mine. It might be easier for you if I told you I had a brutal, abusive childhood, or if I was moulded this way by neglectful parents or a husband who beat me senseless. You might find it easier to comprehend if I had been driven mad with grief by the loss of a child or endured endless cycles of poverty and torment. You might feel less uncomfortable if you could understand or pin a reason on why I did it. But I haven't experienced any more hardship than most. My mundane existence was rather comfortable, nothing out of the ordinary. I was never marked out as the 'problem child' or tearaway; I rarely broke the rules. I didn't torture animals or self-harm when I was a kid. My habits were no unhealthier than yours. You'll scout over all the details of how, when, who and still be left wondering why.

I did something you could never imagine doing and that is what puts me on the other side of the wall from you. Not just a hard stone wall but a fragile wall of glass, cold to the touch and, for now, uncracked.

MYRRH

Myrrh thought about how branches of trees in the wind were like hair, but when it was calm those same branches looked like pencil sketches of capillaries in a dissected heart or lungs. *We are trained to look at the surface and make assumptions on how things appear,* she thought. *We notice the cute button noses and skin tone; we congratulate friends on shedding pounds of flesh or having their hair cut and styled by a stranger; our eyes flick towards big tits or fat buttocks or bushy eyebrows or scars without even knowing we are doing it.* All these noticeable things, these superficial things.

On the journey back to the coast she stopped at a petrol station because, although her fuel light had not reminded her that fuel was low, she liked to plan ahead and be prepared so she would not be put in a situation where, heaven forbid, she was stranded on an unfamiliar road with no means to go forward or back or anywhere at all. Who were these unprepared people who never checked that they had all they needed before a journey, the renegades who spontaneously crashed through life leaping like a monkey swinging from the treetops, barely grasping one vine before reaching towards the next? She needed a level of certainty but secretly admired the messy, chaotic, mindless rushed lives of others.

She picked up her phone to see no new messages, so flicked through the photos from the past few days: the trees, the sunset, a lone figure on a bench looking out to a park, a blurry shot of a house, a street-name sign, the sky above the town and the rooftops dotted with resting pigeons. It all seemed so anonymous, so unfamiliar, so unlike her life by the coast. Did she expect a message from them, from *him*? An apology. Anything?

worthless

useless

She tried to remember the first time she had ever seen the sea and recalled it as a sound like trees in a storm, mingled with a scent like all things dead and alive at the same time, a preserved living-dead thing, and she felt drawn to it, but also wary of it; and there were spaces between the sounds, little pauses, like the white spaces between text on the pages of a book. And she wondered why people spoke of the sea like it was calming and restorative when it mostly destroyed things in it, on it or beside it, how it was filled with creatures munching their way through each other, currents grinding and crushing and mashing in an endless briny cycle.

When she returned home, she didn't know whether she would tell anyone about what happened. Switching to practical matters, quantifying the trouble and upheaval of changing who she was, who she had grown attached to, but realising it meant nothing to anyone else. Didn't everyone have a terribly complex backstory of their own? A life filled with stuff you just didn't talk about?

As the fuel filled up in her tank she watched as an estate car, full of family, pull up to the pump beside her: two adults, two children, a bootful of holiday belongings crammed against the rear windscreen. One of the kids, a young girl of about ten, stared at her from the backseat. Myrrh looked away, then back again, ready to offer a smile, but the girl poked out her tongue and wrinkled up her nose. The girl had red hair and freckles that would've been brought out by the sun as she clambered over rockpools or darted in and out of the surf, ignoring her mother's pleas of 'Not too far,' or 'Don't go in too deep'.

'That's not what I meant…' The mother's voice sliced the air like sharpened fingernails as she stepped from the driver's seat and slammed her car door. The young girl in the backseat continued staring out her window at Myrrh.

The man in the front passenger seat sat motionless yet full of suppressed explosives. Myrrh imagined that inside him was a battalion of armour-plated locusts ready to spew out of his mouth, but he kept it shut because if he dared open it to speak the locusts would burst free and strip all the flesh off his wife, leaving her as just a pile of bones on the forecourt in front of her screaming children. *That is why he remains silent*, Myrrh thought, *and why he keeps very still, because if he moves there is a possibility everyone will die and it would be on his conscience that he had let the killer locusts out to do what killer locusts do best.*

Myrrh looked up at the flickering display of numbers on the petrol pump, aware of the oily scent filling her nostrils. On the surface, she probably appeared well-adjusted, rational, diplomatic even, but the goblin knew otherwise. She realised then that if she were that other woman – the mother of that family – driving home from a short holiday, she might consider driving herself and her offspring and husband, with his latent flesh-eating locust tendencies, off a cliff and down to the unforgiving rocks below.

Goblin smirked

Myrrh thought of all the people she'd like to put in the car with her if she were to drive off that cliff onto the rocks below and decided she'd need a bigger vehicle and wouldn't it just be an act of kindness rather than murder, and through death she'd be associated with them forever, when in life she hadn't been and the cruel irony of it all.

Goblin cackled

And Myrrh thought that one spontaneous act of passionate murder would not be enough to portray how much those people, who she had chosen to die with rather than have the choice to live with, had fucked up her life, and perhaps a more direct act, like stabbing or strangling or bashing their skulls in with a tin of baked beans, would be a more satisfying course of action.

The petrol pump noisily clicked and kicked back against her hand. She drew a breath to remove herself from her train of thought and finished paying at the pump. The woman from the estate car emerged from the kiosk, jogged quickly to the car, and launched plastic bottles of cola and bags of snacks onto her husband's lap as she got back in the driver's seat and started the engine.

pour it in their car
douse them with it
burn them all

Myrrh watched that family drive away toward their own cliff and their own rocks. She thought about their shared DNA and the inexplicable link between the girl's red hair and the mother's red hair and the constellation of freckles on their cheeks and their eyes, noses, mouths and those shapes that connected them. And she thought of the ways her own family tried to make those physical connections that were not there, grasping at the ungraspable, pressing heavily on jigsaw pieces with the wrong edges to try and make them fit, knowing that there was no way they would fit, because they were from different jigsaws with different-shaped pieces. But they carried on believing there was a connection because, if they didn't, what or who would stop the goblins breaking free and wreaking havoc with cars and knives and tins of baked beans.

'Please,' she said to Goblin. 'Please stop.'
burn them all
burn it all down

CAYENNE

It all starts with a look. His eyes are not as dark as mine. We are different creatures. However, I know we will end up together. Fate. He is the one who lifts me up from the gutter and I cling on to that hope. Those long lingering gazes as if we can read each other's minds. Caught in a whirlwind, feet-sweeping exhilaration. His attention excites me, the way he sticks his nails under mine when we hold hands, the lingering squeeze of his hand on my thigh, always at each other's side. I want to breathe him in, to consume him. I want to feel the cut and burn of his promises on my body.

He keeps me poised on a precipice. *You'll never want for anything. You are the love of my life. We will live happily ever after.* He has all the silky, smooth words to wrap us up in.

Princess. He rarely uses my actual name. I am his princess. Does that make him my prince? Or my knight in shining armour, saving this damsel in distress from her predicament? It's all twinkly lights and forest glades. It's soft moonlight and skin.

MYRRH

When Myrrh was a teenager, she thought of all the things she would like to shout at her birth mother when they eventually met. Her moods ricocheted between longing and rage, fictitious meetings like those sickly reunion programmes she found difficult to watch on television. She became the adopted daughter she was expected to be, and each time she moved further away from her beginning she felt that ugly churning prompted by the goblin. On top of all the troubles heaped on her teenage self, confusion spilled down her cheeks in hot tears of unspoken angst towards her biological mother:

Why did you not plan your future? My future? Why did you not keep me? Why did you not have an abortion? Do you love me? I don't love you. I don't care if you're dead. I won't know when you die. You are not my relation. Who are you anyway? I am your child. I am not your child. I'm not sorry for the choices you have made that omit me. You are everything I expected and more. You are a disappointment. Why did you sleep with him? Why is it not black and white? Am I black or white? Why can't you fit the picture I have of you in my mind? Do you think of me? Where have you been? Have you tried to find me? Where is my father? Who is he? Why didn't you stay together? Who is he with now who fulfils him in ways that you never did? Where do I come from? Who the fuck am I?

CAYENNE

'Yes,' I gasp. He is holding my face in his hands and I am crying happy tears. The question is barely out of his mouth before he receives my answer. 'Yes,' I say again and kiss him.

I am surprised but try not to let the gratitude dip into desperation. He wipes the tears from my cheeks with his thumbs. I feel his rough skin graze against mine.

'You are happy I asked, aren't you?' he asks.

I kiss him over and over on his lips, his face, the palms of his hands.

'I'm more than happy,' I tell him. 'It's a dream come true.' Am I acting too needy?

Is it a dream? This man is asking me to be part of his family. All of us together. Me, him, his daughter, a family. It's all I've ever wanted. I look around the room and have already decided what colour to repaint the walls. I have already catalogued in my mind the things that must go.

CAYENNE

'Have you been in my room?' she asks.

'No,' I reply and turn to face her. She has a peachy doll face that helps her get away with far too much. But there is a hard edge there. She gets that from her father.

'Oh right, funny...' She sniffs and wipes the back of her hand across her button nose. 'My hairbrush has moved.'

Is she accusing me of something?

'Are you accusing me of moving your stuff?' I ask. It comes out too harsh so I laugh to soften the words, make light of it. But inside my tummy turns on itself.

'Just wondered,' she says. She is sidling around the kitchen, moving ornaments from the dresser and tracing her fingers along the shelves before inspecting them. She inhales long and loud. 'Those flowers look rank.' She gestures to the row of pelargoniums I have added to the windowsills.

'I think they brighten up the place.' I won't let her dampen my mood.

'It's like an old people's home.' She doesn't laugh and slumps down at the kitchen table.

I carry on stirring the sauce in the pan. She is happy enough to eat what I cook every night and leave her soiled empty plate on the table for me to clear up after her.

'When's Dad home?' she asks.

'I'm not sure,' I say. But when I turn she is gone and the sauce has split. I'll have to start over.

CAYENNE

I wake from a fitful sleep feeling despondent, my insides thick with uncertainty and gloom. It is my birthday. You'd think by now he wouldn't need reminding. He needs at least three months' notice. I tear open the envelope and fake a smile. A large, embossed, puke-inducing card: To The One I Love, I Love You With All My Heart, blah blah blah. Maybe he does actually love me, but he hasn't had the forethought or stamina to give me what I really want.

He hands me a weak cup of tea then limply wraps his arms around my waist. I endure this for several seconds then twist out of his embrace, faking a coughing fit.

He must know something is wrong, but it is futile to put into words how I feel. I get the same old nagging feeling that my life might be heading for a cliff edge, especially now I have broached the difficult question of us having a child together. Time is not on my side. I want to be in love; I want the fairytale; I need the happily ever after. A flare of anger lights up my cheeks as I think how much we have to depend on men to give this to us. One small thrusting act of pleasure and their part in the story can end if they so wish.

It is my birthday. There will be booze and with any luck I can drink until I pass out and we will fumble in the dark until we are both sticky and spent from our exertions and maybe, just maybe, I will conceive.

MYRRH

Mrs Mackman saw in the child a part of her that wanted to run like a wild horse, nostrils flaring, hot steam escaping from her lungs. Her will was like steel, like petrol to a flame.

'That baby is like a symphony,' she would remark. 'I've seen enough of them come and go.'

She'd scoop her up in her arms but found it difficult to contain the wriggling, all arms and legs pumping as if she were a piston engine, as if she were trying to escape. It was as if the child needed to move or would seize up, turn to stone.

There were times when she truly thought these children that came and went were part of her clan. Places were always laid at the table just as she laid George's place when he was at sea. A superstitious fisherman's wife was how she thought others regarded her. She couldn't have been further from the truth. She was admired for all she did with those waifs and strays. She was the temporary lifebuoy for those stormy lives.

'What's expected will come to those who wait.' Her determined but kind voice seemed to soothe those wayward souls much as she'd done for her own flesh and blood.

Mrs Mackman would sing in a voice – sweet and light – that didn't quite fit with her solid, rotund body. She produced an upbeat melodic sound that warmed the small cottage where hundreds

POLLY HALL

of children had passed through, anticipating love, unaware of their fate, waiting for parents or guardians to take them to a forever home.

She only sang when no one else was in the room with her. Her voice carried like a siren's call. As if she sang secrets of the deep. She knew the sea and how it could take her husband from her in an instant with no warning. Her superstitions grew larger at night-time when George was out on a late tide. That was why she busied herself with the children. They were her mainstay, with their funny little patterns, the ebb and flow of their instincts.

'I worry about them all,' she explained to her friend and neighbour, Mrs Willows. 'But she's different. I don't know how to explain it.'

'A bit odd?' Mrs Willows offered unhelpfully while looking over at the row of nap cloths drying by the fire then back at the baby, who nuzzled a bottle and wrinkled up its tiny features. *It could be a changeling*, she thought. *A fairy child. A creature from another world.* She could tell its skin was darker than the others but made no comment.

'No, not odd. Just different, more aware.'

There had been a hold up with paperwork so they'd called her up for an emergency placement, short-term foster care. Plenty of new parents waiting, though, they told her as they bundled the tiny infant into her arms with only her hospital clothes and nothing more. She didn't doubt it. But there were plenty of parentless children too.

Mrs Mackman shared tea and scones with a few of her friends as part of a ritual to dilute the daily chores with what she liked to call a 'sit-down'. She had been taking in children for years, some damaged beyond repair even when she mined the well of her compassion, to soak them with love until they were packed off to some other foster home or, on occasions, placed with a suitable family. It was best not to keep mementoes or dwell on the tears and tantrums.

'I don't normally let them get to me,' she told Mrs Willows one afternoon. 'Would you call me sentimental?'

Mrs Willows shook her head. 'Not you,' she said. 'No, not sentimental at all.'

George was not due home until the early morning, and she knew she would not sleep. His absence coincided with a new boy joining the household. He had 'significant problems with truancy', the social worker had reminded her. Mrs Mackman had nodded and smiled. *Running away was not an issue*, she thought. *It was what you were running towards that seemed to cause most hassle.*

Most of them were masters at manipulation, vying for attention in the hope that it would reap a reward or two. It never worked. She treated each one of them fairly, and they soon got to learn that she would not budge in her opinion or routine. It was her house and her rules. That said, Mrs Mackman would accept their little gifts honestly and sincerely: a posy of wilting weeds, a bow tie fashioned from a used crisp wrapper or, at Easter time, painted crosses or decorated eggs they'd bring home from school classes. But after they had left her home, she'd carefully untack the paper art from the walls and doors or lift the dusty craftwork from her shelves and incinerate them in the garden, watching black flecks of ash disintegrate before her eyes. It was best that way: to move on and make way for the new.

She cleared the mugs and went out to the garden to retrieve the washing from the line. Two children – only six and seven, a brother and sister – were due home from school. It was a fair day, but she would still listen to the shipping forecast later, religiously, as a habit. She didn't really understand the rise and fall but liked to hear the names meditatively pronounced: Fitzroy, Rockall, German Bight. She pretended they were mythical creatures being conjured up from deep beneath the ocean.

The baby girl was sleeping in her crib now. She slept all day mostly. At night she lay awake staring at the ceiling watching out for some unseen thing, eyes wide and glistening as she bawled in that spectral way babies do. No amount of soothing or milk seemed to placate her during the wee small hours. She had a look like she'd been here before, that she knew some unspeakable thing but could not yet verbalise it. Her tiny fists were bunched up in cotton mittens that seemed a little pointless, her cheeks already covered in scratches. While trimming her nails to the quick Mrs Mackman could've sworn the baby uttered profanities, sounds emerging like wicked swear words that would even make her fisherman husband blush. But the child was far too young to speak. She was only a babe not long out of the womb, bless her poor soul.

Mrs Mackman turned on the wireless and caught the end of the news, shock in a small town, a young pregnant woman was missing, and the newsreaders spoke about neighbours fearing for her safety and the safety of her unborn child.

CAYENNE

I tread on eggshells. I change my plans. I shapeshift into their life.

She lays it on thick that she is his only daughter, his only family. Just because you are related to someone doesn't mean you own them.

'You may resent me because your father loves me. He says he loves me more than anything. More than you? Would you ever believe it? I naïvely thought we could get along at the start, but I have seen too many times how you try to exclude me. He says you're too unimaginative to do this, but I don't underestimate you the way he does.

'This house is not a home for me while you are in it. The way you childishly sit on his lap even though you are a grown woman; the way you share your thoughts with him while ignoring my direct questions; the way you speak to him in that whiny baby voice. It's all bullshit. Grow up! We have put our plans on hold because of you. I want children. You won't always be his number one.'

Of course, I would never say any of this to her face. It is all holed up inside me like a nest of vipers. Maybe I will have hordes of children with him, all vying for his affections, and she will be snapped up by a man of her own or become the handless maiden. Chop, chop. She cannot remain pure forever. We must all make sacrifices for our family.

At first, he may just forget the little things, like the way she walks or blinks. Then her voice, and, as time passes and our new family begins to edge into his daily life, he will find there are hours, days, weeks when he doesn't think of her at all.

She says she's not fussed by what he does or what I do. In my experience when people say they don't care, they do. A lot.

MYRRH

Myrrh was born on a Thursday *(Thursday's child has far to go)*. Perhaps the childhood saying had a maxim of truth behind its rhyme. She had moved far from her cultural and genetic roots and the hardest part was letting go of that fact. She tenaciously held onto the belief that the answer to her nature lay in the unknown past. Perhaps it meant the journey was to return to the start, like the pilgrim who travelled across many lands to seek his treasure when all along it was buried beneath his feet. If she held on to that belief, something like an invisible thread tightened around her will, as if she were being pulled back to the beginning. She felt like a child in a fairytale using breadcrumbs to find her way back home, only to realise she was not only lost but hungry too.

Summer suited her. She could blossom and express her fullness, her smile radiant and her body melting the constriction of the cold, dark winter months. Born in August, at the height of summer in a year that blistered and crackled from excessive heat, there seemed to be a rigidity set in her, like the apparent dryness of a desert. Like the desert, she housed beauty and terror in many guises.

When she turned nine, her parents organised a birthday party. Sandwiches made from gluey white bread. Sickly iced cupcakes piled onto plates. Jelly and ice cream slopped into bowls. And curly worm-like crisps stained lips and fingers with orange dust.

It was a small affair with mainly friends from her neighbourhood. If she knew at that age the path that lay ahead, would she have allowed herself to enjoy that moment? It was a party, not a wake, but she was constantly anticipating drama, a broken glass slicing through tender skin or someone feeling left out during the games and the incessant malevolent whisper of the goblin

this will never last, this will never last
bite your tongue and fill your mouth with blood
stuff it in
stuff it down
choke on it

The plates smeared with half-eaten sponge cake were stacked by the kitchen sink, jam tarts scattered like Alice in Wonderland extras across the lawn. Myrrh had said goodbye to her friends and sat alone on her bed feeling sick. She thought it was from too much cake, but as she drew her knees up to her chest there was something else bothering her insides. She rushed to the toilet and threw up.

you can't squash me down
I'll always be here
I am meant to be here

She retched but there was nothing more to come up. Flecks of her birthday party spattered the toilet bowl.

Did these creatures taunt everyone? And where had he come from? Was that the moment she realised she was cursed?

CAYENNE

I am feeling gracious. Overwhelming generosity flows out of me. I decide to talk with his daughter to find common ground. I feel we can work on our complicated relationship. It is all I've ever wanted. I know I am not perfect, but I want her to see I am human, that I have feelings too. I will never be her mother, she will never be my daughter, but perhaps there is a chance we can work something out.

Our conversation goes something like this:

Me: I'd like to talk to you. When are you free? Tonight?
Her: No. Maybe tomorrow.
Me: Okay. Let's talk tomorrow, have a proper conversation.
Her: Whatever.

This is what annoys the hell out of me: her apparent indifference and the certainty that she will win whatever battle she thinks we are fighting. Does she know the leverage she has over her father is stronger than mine ever will be? I am powerless to exert any control over the situation unless I change my mindset.

I am not her parent, but I have been thrown into this role. My words bounce off her, we speak in foreign tongues, her words, my words, all layered together and incoherent. I try to say, 'I'm here for you.' She does not need me. She will never need me. One motherless child speaking to another motherless child about something neither of us understand.

Is it easier if the child is from your womb?

MYRRH

There must've been a first time her tongue recorded the moment when the sweetness tricked her into thinking it was good for her. Now nostalgia would seep down her throat whenever she twisted the wrapper. It was too tempting to just suck the sweet, to delay its dissolving pleasure, so she'd crunch it, letting fragments mould into her teeth like temporary fillings.

'Caramel?' Myrrh asked. Her therapist raised his eyebrows as she tried to explain. That was what the memory tasted like. He said that all the senses must be employed to fully experience the memory, so she latched upon caramel. It sounded as dreamy as its taste.

'Am I cursed?' she asked him.

'Cursed? How?'

'Because I didn't have a choice. My fate was already decided.'

'That's the same for all of us when we're born.'

'But not everyone is given away, adopted. Not everyone has a mum, dad, brother or sister out there somewhere they know nothing about.'

'Can I ask what is stopping you from finding them, if you wanted to?'

She thought about the tin in the wardrobe at the house she grew up in. That treasure trove of history and information. Right there for her. But then she heard the goblin, his voice growing stronger and stronger

you know nothing
you are nothing
little orphan girl
given up
thrown away
take his pen and stab him in the eye
watch him bleed
make him see

and stronger still the closer the truth got. No. She couldn't go back there. Not yet.

Myrrh gazed around the room and her eyes settled on a painting on the wall. It was a surreal image: a wheel in the centre crossed like a compass with symbols she did not recognise. Stationed at the surrounding edges were mythical creatures – a griffin, and a winged cow and lion, and an angel – all holding books. A sphinx crouched at the top cradling a sword, and a snake was entwined down the left side of the wheel. Below, almost in the same shade of orange as the wheel and shaped around the edge of the painting, was a human figure with the head of a dog, like the depictions she had seen of ancient Egyptian gods.

'What is it meant to be?'

Myrrh studied the image, imagining this woman painting each design, dreaming up something new from old wisdom.

'This one is the Wheel of Fortune,' he said. 'Fate. You can find a lot of symbolism in the artwork.'

Fate as a wheel, thought Myrrh. Always ready to off-road towards you and smack you down flat. What if her fate was to never know where she had come from, who she was?

'It's from the major arcana. These are archetypes. We all have elements of the cards playing out in our lives: new beginnings, disaster, trauma, healing... I'd like to study them more in my work. The Fool's Journey.'

disaster

trauma

'The Fool's Journey?'

'It's all the initiations and pathway we take in life, the ups and downs...'

'Who painted it?'

'Pamela Colman Smith. She was the original artist commissioned to paint the cards by a mystic and poet. She designed and painted seventy-eight cards of the deck.'

Myrrh looked again at the vibrant colours and imagined this woman painting, alone. Each dream-like image conjured from the imagination onto paper.

'Where are the original paintings now?' The passing of time, all that effort buried or broken, moved or displaced by other peoples' actions.

'No one knows; everything was sold when she died. She had a house in Cornwall.' Cornwall. Her birth mother's address. They both stood in front of the painting in silence observing the vibrancy as it danced and merged. *Broken or displaced*, she thought. Could people be broken like objects?

your mother didn't want you

your mother didn't want you

Goblin was awake. She was thinking about her birth mother again, about what she looked like, who she was.

who are you?

you are nobody

a motherless loser

no one named you

name me name me name me

'Shut up!' Myrrh realised she had said this out loud and looked at her therapist to see him raise an eyebrow at her outburst.

'Sad really,' he continued to explain the painter's life. 'She died penniless and alone. Perhaps we never really know our legacy, or our curses. Pixie, they called her.'

Myrrh imagined a small, spritely woman leaning attentively over her desk, paint pots scattered about, vibrant colours splashed on her smock. *She could even be my distant relation*, she thought, *like the man on the bus, a stranger in the supermarket queue, a famous actress*. Then she shrugged off that idea. She couldn't be related to everyone she didn't know. She made a mental note to purchase a pack of the Rider-Waite cards he was talking about.

When she got home she searched 'Pamela Colman Smith' and 'Cornwall' on the internet. There was an address, 'Bencoolen House, Bude, Cornwall'. The more she read about Pamela, the more she was intrigued. She was an artist, deemed by some to be exotic-looking, and her features from the black-and-white photographs corroborated the descriptions. She wore the bohemian-style robes of an eccentric, her hair tied up in a wild bundle on her head, eyes bright as a shard of obsidian.

Cornwall: her birthplace. That was what she'd been told. The paintings, the cards: it all felt like fate. Maybe she could travel to Cornwall.

What did she know? Her mother's name and her putative father's name as stated on the copy of her birth certificate. Their dates of birth and the address of her birth mother at that time. It wasn't that far from where she lived now. Cornwall: land of legend. She had holidayed there among the clotted cream, pasties and enormous seagulls. It felt familiar. Maybe she could slot the missing pieces together if she returned to her roots. And then, as quick as the idea came to her

what makes you think you are wanted?
no one wants damaged goods
you weren't wanted then

you aren't wanted now
As she left, she slammed the door harder than was necessary
to drown out goblin's whiny taunts.

CAYENNE

I have started talking to the spider in the kitchen. When I flick on the kettle she pops out of a crack by the edge of the tiles and pauses until I speak. There is a moment when I feel our eyes meet, all the thousands of hers and my two, although I cannot see her eyes. But we have an understanding. I drop a teabag in my mug and open the fridge to retrieve the milk. She twitches then retreats into the crevice. I think she may be hungry. Spiders eat their own, I know that much. But I forget about the tiny creature until I see a young girl in the market.

She dances like a spider down the aisles, scuttling past the frozen peas and crinkle-cut chips until she reaches a display of stacked cereal boxes at the end of the aisle and continues on. She pirouettes by the chocolate bars and bows to the potatoes and onions. An old man selecting an overfilled bag of red apples casts a sidelong glance at her then shuffles off, holding his basket with both hands as if it might contain the answers to all of life's great questions.

The girl's mum rounds the corner, pushing a trolley laden with toilet tissue and bright drinks cartons. 'Sharon – here – now!' she shrieks. The girl skids up to her mum's side and grips the end of the trolley, leaps so both her feet land on the cross bar, and then extends one arm above her head in a grand finale. Her mother grabs the trolley with both hands to stop it tipping and squawks her chastising refrain.

'Full of beans at that age, aren't they?' An older lady strikes up a conversation while smiling at the girl's mother.

'Something like that.' She huffs a reply and waves her hand at her daughter as if batting away a pestering insect. 'Stop that!' she snaps again. The lady purses her lips and moves off, then smiles at the girl who is blissfully unaware of her audience, her mother or anyone else. She retrieves a bag of crisps as her reward but not before her mother smacks her hand away and the bubble is burst. She is once again a girl in a supermarket with her stressed-out mother under the lurid strip lighting that offers nothing but glaring reality.

It turns out, from a book I discovered in the library, that spiders have a varied diet; they are quite the gourmet of the arachnid world. They have a taste for decomposed insects or fruit flies when they are spiderlings with smaller jaws. They can survive long periods without any food or water, unlike our species. We are weak with our fragile, pierceable skin, leaking blood and dying from the inside out.

As I iron one of his shirts, I notice a lump that might be a knot of thread, but as soon as the heat presses against it there is a small pop like a bubble bursting. I realise I have killed a spider, possibly the spider I have been talking to, by pressing hot plates onto its body. What a death! That popping sound. I can't bring myself to launder the shirt again. I throw it in the trash with the dead spider still welded to the fabric and pretend it never existed.

MYRRH

Breathing in and out, in and out. In through the nose, out through the mouth. Mantras of meditation invisibly flowed from blocked nostrils in a dusty room. Myrrh thought at first she might laugh so squinted her eyes shut to concentrate on the in-breath and the out-breath as instructed. Meditation. *Med-it-ation. Med-it-ation*. It proved a lot harder than it sounded. Her mind was like a caged wild cat wanting to break free and chase the nearest moving object. It erratically darted between the trivia of the day: a conversation she had earlier with a resident at the care home where she worked, her shopping list, the woman with crazy hair she had passed in the street screeching obscenities at her own reflection in a shop window.

They always started with a short meditation. Heather, the group leader, said it was better if everyone tried to relax before tuning in to each other's auras. Auras: layers around the physical, depicted as halos in old oil paintings, mystical cloaks of lights, awe-inspiring visions. Were they not supposed to be sensed as you would sense a person pressing close to you? Were they just another mystery to unravel?

Myrrh had talked to friends about auras as if she were talking about her eyes or her hair and caught a snigger from… she couldn't remember who now, but there had been a deep sense of being

38

misunderstood rising like bile in her throat. She was always more aware that something lay beneath the surface, a story behind the story.

She'd sat confused during all those Sunday-school lessons when no one batted an eyelid if the Virgin Mary or the Three Wise Kings following a star from the East or the Angel Gabriel was referred to in passing conversation, like they were chatting about a visit to the supermarket or what they had eaten for dinner the night before last. It was thoroughly confusing to look upon those images of exotic, silk-clad men upon camels and find any connection to her life in a sleepy, rural English town. Yet she felt somehow internally connected to these images of desert and dark-skinned travellers. Although she tried her hardest to fit in, she felt she would always be searching for that missing part of herself.

Now Myrrh was partnered with Colin. His breath smelt like tinned fish and vinegar and she wasn't sure she could sit next to him without gagging, but he kept moving his chair nearer to hers every time she shuffled backwards, and if she carried on shifting away from him she would be trapped in the corner. He breathed through his mouth and she could hear his tongue clacking with dried spit. He kept grinning at her with an eagerness she associated with desperation, so she smiled back, not wanting to offend him and reminded herself that, as Heather put it, *all beings are special, all beings are worthy of non-judgement.*

The group was open to all ages, but looking round the room she estimated she brought down the average age by at least twenty years; she was yet again positioned as the odd one out.

'Love and light to you all,' Heather said, 'Now we are going to do a reading for each other using tarot cards. I know some of you have brought your own packs, but if you'd like to borrow some, I have a few packs here.'

Colin took a pack and shuffled his cards poorly. They kept

falling out of his hands, flipping over and landing on his lap or slipping between his legs to the floor. He'd scrabble to pick them up, bending them and creasing them, his awkwardness making Myrrh more and more uncomfortable. She was glad she hadn't brought her own Colman-Smith pack; they were too precious to share with the group. It was as if she felt the energy from them would be tainted, the magic lost if anyone else touched them.

'We are going to do a three-card spread.' Heather was gliding around the room like a stately bird on a lake, wafting the scent of patchouli each time she moved.

'Think of a question.' Colin grinned at Myrrh, his lips riding up over his gums. She could think of several at that moment, but she thought of the most current question, the question that was always whirring around her head like a wasp at a picnic.

don't say it
don't you dare
can of worms
slimy worms in your mouth

'I'd like to know how to find my family.'

Colin snorted. 'What – lost them have you?'

lost and found
worms in the ground
worms in your mouth

He looked up at her face and must have felt the ferocity in her stare from his flippant comment because he stopped grinning and noisily swallowed his spit.

'Rightio – okay then.' He tapped the cards on the table and placed them face down in front of Myrrh.

'Cut three times,' he said.

cut and slice
slit it open

She split the pack three times, each time placing the bottom pile back on top. He rubbed his hands together as if warming them up to touch someone else's skin. Myrrh couldn't imagine him being intimate with anyone; he had hairs poking out of his nose, with one thick black hair vibrating each time he breathed out, like an insect leg trying to escape from a crevice. Myrrh looked down at the cards and tried to concentrate.

'Remember when you interpret the cards, your words hold power.' Heather swept past again like a contestant in a dance show. Everyone looked up each time she said something, hanging on her words, not wanting to make a metaphysical cock-up.

Myrrh selected three cards and placed them face down on the table between them. Colin rubbed his hands together while muttering, 'Situation, Action, Outcome.' There they were neatly lined up with their backs to her, ready to be revealed. An answer to her question?

no one cares
lost forever

'First card. Ready?' Colin started grinning again. He turned it over. 'Reversed Emperor. Okay, I'll just check my notes.' He pulled some scraps of paper out of his trouser pocket and studied them for a moment. 'It could mean a new life or an immaturity of sorts. Does that make any sense?'

'I suppose so,' Myrrh said, not having a clue what he was talking about. When she thought of an emperor she regarded an austere man, mature in his years and sure of his authority.

daddy's little girl
daddy doesn't care

Goblin stirred and dug an elbow into her liver

daddy hates your liver
daddy hates your guts

'Oh – I know!' Suddenly with all the answers, Colin lunged forward. 'It could mean that you have to make some hard decisions, but you are finding it difficult to do so.' He looked pleased with himself. 'Next card?' His hand hovered over the middle card.

'Ooh another reversed card, Myrrh, look, it's the High Priestess this time. So… erm… we are looking at 'Action' this time. Rightio…'

'Try and not rely too much on your notes, everyone,' Heather spoke as Colin flicked frantically through the pages of his notebook. He placed it on his lap and closed his eyes. Myrrh felt like rolling hers but sat back instead to listen. She could tell Goblin was enjoying the uncertainty writhing in her guts.

stab him in the head
gouge out his tongue

'Ok, let's tune in,' he said. 'Reversed High Priestess.' She imagined the image of the High Priestess upended with her head stuck in the sand, all her robes tangled up in her veil, legs ungainly wobbling in the air. When she'd got her own cards, she studied each one, letting the colours and unusual images soak into her as if she could feel their meaning.

'This is a card about mystery, about the unseen…' Colin was on a roll now. 'But reversed it could mean that you are afraid to open up to others.'

open it up
slice it clean

'I've always felt I was quite open about everything.' It sounded defensive even to her own ears as she blurted it out. If she were honest, she was always afraid to open up to others; her inability to place full trust in others was becoming more and more evident. Her stomach made a grumbling noise, and she instinctively placed the palm of her hand over it. The goblin was growing impatient.

open the door
trip trap across the threshold
unbox the secrets

Heather stood behind Colin, momentarily putting him into suspended animation. 'Carry on as if I'm not here,' she whispered to the back of his head. He swallowed noisily and started waffling. 'The High Priestess reversed means you could become too involved in something, you could lose yourself in it.'

'Or it could mean—' Heather stepped in '—that someone is not taking action when she should be. Is there something you are wanting to do, Myrrh, perhaps searching for something but not knowing how to go about it?'

I can twist your guts so they make you shit out your mouth
your shitty words will spew out
you're the dirty little secret
think you know the truth, do you?

Myrrh felt heat rise up her neck. Heather had nailed it. She was delaying the actual search for the truth about her birth, worrying too much about the outcome, and preventing herself from getting on with it out of fear. Fear of hurting her adoptive mother and father, fear of being hurt herself, fear of the unknown, fear of giving more power to goblin.

guess my name
name me
you'll never guess it

'The unknown is only scary because we haven't been there,' Heather said softly then moved on to the next couple staring at the cards in front of them.

'Outcome!' Colin turned the third card. Myrrh had a feeling it would not be a sunny card like the Empress or the Magician. She glimpsed the black image on the card before he finished turning it. 'The Devil. Rightio, not to worry,' he said, making her even more worried. 'I'm sure it's not too bad as this one's reversed, too. How odd, eh? All standing on their head, Myrrh. Ha ha. Yes. OK... let's talk about the Devil then.'

But there wasn't time. Heather was getting the group to swap partners so Myrrh left Colin swallowing his spit and muttering about devils and how nothing is as bad as it seems.

She thought about all the choices her mother had made in her life. Was placing her child for adoption a choice? What had she been told? That her mother had been distressed, the father of the unborn child not on the scene, and her life lined up as a single parent at that time would not have been easy. She tried to put herself in her mother's shoes for just a moment, but it still made her feel conflicted and confused. Mothers were supposed to fight for you, to cling to you in every circumstance no matter how terrifying or stressful. Weren't mothers supposed to love you right from the moment they felt the quickening in their womb?

guess my name, witch
if you guess it, I'll let you know a secret
but if you don't…
I get to take what's yours

CAYENNE

'Just thought I'd phone because y'know…'

I know.

'You don't want to talk?' he says.

'I do.'

'Well?' he asks. His voice a sharp edge of impatience.

'I just want to say…' I want to tell him that I want us to be parents. But I hardly have time to compose myself because these are words that need to be spoken face to face while looking into each other's eyes like they do in the movies, music heightening to provide dramatic emphasis, the male lead taking the female lead and sweeping her into a loving embrace, him saying, *yes-yes, a thousand times yes* and *I love you more than anything.*

'Say what? Cayenne, I'm busy. What do you want to talk about?'

He rarely calls me Princess these days.

'Oh… It's nothing.'

'For fuck's…'

He hangs up.

MYRRH

Some days Myrrh would wake light as papyrus until she reinhabited her body from the lucid dreams that seemed so real. Then, with a heavy clod of earth placed upon her back and shoulders, she'd deflate, brought back down to reality.

There'd been occasions in her life when she dreamed of being airborne, not with wings, but in a sort of elevated prone pose, a child playing at aeroplanes or a superhero flying through the sky. She'd mentally will herself to lift from the ground and raise her body higher until she was looking down at fields and trees, always wanting to reach a destination but never quite making it before the shrill alarm by her bedside jolted her from the fuzziness of her nightscape.

After waking, her limbs felt weighted by lead and she'd keep her eyes tightly shut, wishing she could re-enter the dream space from which she had been torn. Her essence would shift through the seasons, days, hours and even minutes. Alchemical elements – air, fire, earth and water – would merge or slip around her body.

In winter she felt a contraction in her body: ice forming in her veins, then softening, followed by movement like soil massaged by worms as spring emerged abundant and verdant as if by magic. Summer, her favourite season, brought with it the promise of warmth and long days of light before seeping into autumn full of slow sap and the witness of migrating birds that appeared like dust motes in the far-off sky before the ground settled into another revolution of the earth's cycle.

At the end of her shift, she set off on her route along the seafront. Some days the breeze was light, but mostly a sharp cross-wind pushed gulls back inland where they hung on invisible strings above the seawall, scouting for scraps of food. The first sprinkling of tourists had arrived in the Easter break, devouring salty chips and littering the pavements with fried food and wrappers. The gulls dipped and dived greedily, clucking at one another with dirty-white raised wings, their keen eyes homing in on the discarded bounty.

She heard a noise that didn't fit with the sandy brush of waves or the tinkering clash of the amusement arcade merging with children's shouts and squeals. A high-pitched cackle and a mysterious, eerie tune coming towards her. A vehicle slowly approached, pulling a huge cage stationed on the top of a trailer. Seated behind its plastic bars was a warty old hag dressed in black robes and a pointed hat. The music seemed to come from within the mannequin's body, her head set at a jaunty angle where she had slumped sideways from the bumpy movement of the vehicle. A few children shrieked and pointed, but most of the pedestrians carried on walking.

There was something sad about the witch, caged motionless in those bars, that triggered a memory of her grandfather's model cottages that were no longer on display. It could have been the straight lines of the cage that matched the Tudor facades he meticulously crafted from matchsticks, or maybe it was the melancholy, stationery figure that reminded her of the neat little miniature sculptures he had designed with such precision and painted with fine brush strokes. Each windowpane lovingly installed with tweezers and tiny shrubs no larger than the end of a cotton bud. She could imagine herself as a miniature version living there in those sweet little buildings with nothing or nobody to trouble her. But would any space ever be small enough to escape from those feelings of dread when she sensed her goblin stirring?

The stories filling her up and clogging her judgement fed the goblin, which grew stronger year by year. It started as a weight inside her chest then seeped down into her gut, twisting and mangling her organs as it grew.

feed me

feed me more

it wailed. It seemed to not only to want to exist inside her but claim her life as its own. But this was her life, not his. Why should she listen to him goad and belittle her?

The witch drew closer, and its face angled towards Myrrh, revealing sharp, pointed teeth. Myrrh shivered as she watched it pass by. *Just a silly plastic prop*, she thought. But it still made her spine tingle. She recalled witches from her childhood story books: old hags in houses made from sweets and cakes. Why had the children gone deep into the dark wood? Hadn't their parents abandoned them there? Only a useless trail of breadcrumbs to lead them home? She imagined them losing their way over and over. Given up for dead at the mercy of wild beasts with no one to protect them. Wasn't it the witch who offered them shelter? Fed their hungry bellies. And they trusted her. Don't all children trust adults to know best?

you'll never find the truth

but I know it

you took what was mine

feed me

feed me

feed me

moremoremoremore

it hurts but you'll get used to it

Goblin's stories always ended with hunger or pain or gruesome dismembered parts devoured by fire.

you are mine
I hurt you hurt you
What good had he ever done for her?
you need me
feed me
Goblin forced his warped idea of truth into her veins, but it was time to find her own way to it.
you owe me
She had lived long enough with his taunts. No matter what Goblin would do, she was still her own person. She wasn't a caged mannequin like the witch on the back of a trailer. She had her own thoughts, and she had a family who loved and supported her. She felt an intense urge to go to her parents' home and find the old tin of papers in the wardrobe, and she tried to push Goblin back down as far as she could.

CAYENNE

I press the razor against my skin and scrape it from ankle to knee. The blade nicks the part where my knee contours out, and blood blooms into the water. I press hard onto the cut then lick the blood off my finger. It tastes too sweet to be mine. I let the blood trickle down my shin into the bath water. It is not a lot. Far less than when it oozes from me in gelatinous clots.

I can think more clearly when I am alone in the bath. I run my hands across my flat stomach then push it out so it looks round and full. I could harbour a child within my body. I could grow it, mould it, love it. It would be all mine. Something that no one could take away from me.

I want his child. We could be a family. A proper family. His daughter is the fly in the ointment. The dirty spiralling insect spoiling the pure cream of our love. I want to scream in her face.

Time is running out and I need a child, my own child. I need him. I need his child. Or do I? Perhaps I just need a child of my own? If I cannot have his, and we cannot be a family, then I could leave.

There are things I can leave behind if I have to make a quick exit. I'm not attached to things, not really; I already got rid of a lot when I left my former life. If I decide to leave, I will not stay in this miserable country. I'll move to Paris or Berlin, or even travel for a bit. I've always wanted to travel, to see the world, to sleep on beaches and watch the sunrise, to hang out with the bohemians in after-hours clubs drinking gin and talking Balzac. I've always wanted to share that with a loving partner. I might meet the man of my dreams who doesn't have children or baggage and who maybe has the time and freedom to start a new family with me. Will jealousy still hound me? Maybe this provincial life isn't the one for me after all if I'm thinking like this.

All these thoughts stick in me like pins. They stab at me but leave no visible scars. Am I trapped in this invisible cage of domesticity? If I stay? Consequences: I must put up with his daughter. I must bite my tongue. I must forfeit all my freedoms. I must step into the wicked-stepmother role. I must stay with him for security. I must get pregnant as soon as possible. I must get pregnant by any means. I need a baby more than I need air. Women get pregnant all the time. Why can't it happen to me? What's wrong with me? Am I cursed?

MYRRH

'Mum,' she called as she let herself in through the back door. It was rarely locked. No one answered, so she kicked off her shoes and rushed upstairs. The blood in her head pumping in rhythm with her heartbeat. The cat lay neatly curled on the corner of her parents' bed, tail tucked under its front paws. When Myrrh reached to stroke its fur, it strained a half mew then started purring rhythmically. It had been so long since she had rifled through her parents' wardrobe in search of her adoption paperwork. And now, as she sat on the bed looking at the wardrobe, a hint of nausea swept upwards. It was as if she were burgling her own identity, stealing it back from a hidden place among the jumpers and shirts. She opened one of the cupboard doors, and a ball of socks leapt out and rolled past her feet. She quickly grabbed it and stuffed it back in the place from where it had launched itself, and her fingers met a cool, metallic surface among the soft wool.

As Myrrh grew, all she was really trying to do was expunge the monster of doubt and shame that had been left inside her. The goblin wailing and grasping at any passing jot of love.

love me, love me

it screamed, grappling with a begging bowl in which to catch scraps of affection. No amount of love was enough. The goblin never matured. It just festered like a sick mass of deep yearning, gnawing away at her. She thought about talking to it sometimes but didn't see the point. It could be vile and taunting, neglectful and indifferent, needy then spiteful, shifting moods so suddenly she felt battered inside and out.

you are useless
I hate you
I love you
love me
name me

Her doubts and fears bubbled up from the tin of secrets in her parents' wardrobe. She carefully dislodged it from the mountain of socks and laid it out on the bed. The lid of the tin rested on top of one of her grandfather's miniature cottages, which itself was acting as a paperweight for the small pile of papers. She lifted it out and examined the delicate intricacies of his handiwork, each roof tile gleaming with glossy red paint, each window a delicate shining square glinting like a diamond, and a door, meticulously hinged with a tiny metal wire so it opened with a welcoming squeak. The little houses were a symbol of his quiet, supportive love as her grandfather, his dedication displayed in miniature form.

Myrrh put it aside and carefully lifted the pile of tatty papers from the tin, holding the top sheet closer to her face and inhaling its old scent. It was a newspaper cutting of a personal notice column with faded small print.

'We are delighted to welcome our granddaughter to our family. Not born to us but loved dearly as our own. Granny and Granddad.'

Tears welled up in Myrrh's eyes and she watched the cat lift its head, stretch out its paw, yawn then settle back down. Her adoptive family had welcomed her with no judgement, and, as such, Myrrh expected unconditional love from all other strangers, too. A catastrophic expectation for even the most lovable creature.

But while her adoptive parents' love was strong, no amount of sticking plaster could keep her from feeling useless, a mere replica of the original, like a miniature cottage only fit for display purposes, never to be lived in.

Sometimes, when she could sense the spotlight on her, the chasm between the known and unknown was more visible. Birthdays were the worst kind of spotlight. An anniversary of celebration versus an anniversary of loss and sorrow.

She shuffled through the other old pieces of paper then shoved them all back in the tin. Something squirmed inside her like a pit of snakes, and bile threatened to rise up to her throat.

you are not the chosen one
pick me
name me

A sharp high-pitched voice pierced her head.

who do you think you are?

Goblin. That's what she had named that unwanted voice the first time she heard it. When she was a child she read about the little people who lived beyond the veil in fairyland: some good, some bad, but all very real to her. She quickly scribbled down scant details from the papers in front of her – unvisited addresses, faceless names – and as she stared again at the faded typed words she heard the click of the latch on the back door, so quickly returned the tin and its contents to the wardrobe.

Goblin puffed up his scrawny chest. Smoke filled her eyes but she wiped away the tears with the back of her hand.

'You're not real!' she said out loud. 'You're nothing.'

so are you

CAYENNE

Who have I been before now? Someone's foundation, someone's door. I lay in bed contemplating my life when it happened. Delicate brushes on my thighs, a gentle warmth through my body as if sinking into a warm bath. At first, I thought perhaps my husband had become possessed by a passion so removed from his usual predictable pattern, but then I sensed it was more than merely physical. An angel – that is how I can only describe what visited me – entered my body and began to make love to me.

When the sensation first overcame me, I found it hard to control my heart, which was pounding so hard in my chest I thought it might burst, but this angel, this ghost lover, whispered unspoken words. It told me not to be afraid, to surrender to the experience. A core of light pulsated over my body, and waves of the most intense pleasure engulfed me. I shook so violently I felt I would wake the idiot snoring beside me, but he remained asleep, completely unaware. I felt no sense of betrayal to him. This was pure and heavenly. My limbs were floating. Swimming freely in the ether. Colours washed me clean. Above me, sky. Below me, forests. And him wrapped around me.

I spent my waking hours wishing the day away so I could slip between the sheets and welcome my ghost lover again.

MYRRH

'Your mum's a proper mum,' Eva, her best friend, commented as they guzzled jelly and ice-cream from bright pink bowls. *A proper mum*, thought Myrrh. A mum who stayed at home, cooked and cleaned, kept the larder stocked full of food and wore canary-yellow rubber gloves and a frilly apron to do the washing up, who wet the corner of her hanky and wiped dirt off cheeks with kind efficiency. Her 'proper' mum taught her how to make pastry and bake cakes; she would gently inspect bruises and read stories, tuck in the bed sheets at night, and leave Post-its in her school lunchbox: *Good luck today, I'll be thinking of you. Lots of Love Mum xx.* Her proper mum would ferry Myrrh and her friends in her Datsun Cherry, stuffed in the back like toys in a box. Myrrh's mum was everyone's mum. The back door was always open, the kettle always filled. She was the best listener and the best tea maker.

Myrrh always thought her skin had been dyed by her mum's tea. The herbal teas fascinated her; she'd let the steam tickle her nostrils and dream of log fires and toasted crumpets. 'It's no trouble,' her mum would say, always self-effacing as though her kindnesses were unworthy of any praise. Myrrh's skin took on varying shades of colour like the tea: milky Earl Grey during the sunless winter months and smoky Lapsang Souchong during the height of summer when the rest of her family turned pink and freckly. She knew then that she was not grown from the same plant. Even so, people would look at her and her dad's dark hair and say, 'That must be where you get it from'. She had always known she was adopted from an early age, so it was amusing when strangers commented on their physical similarities.

With every boyfriend she played a different role, fit into their lives, followed their hobbies, and compromised her own self-development because it was easier to fit into others' self-assured views of the world. She switched hairstyles, fashion, accents, moods: a chameleon adept at suiting any occasion or environment. One boyfriend who particularly liked motorbikes encouraged her to take her test, and she impulsively bought a new motorcycle, scaring the living daylights out of her mum who went on and on about how she had just signed her death warrant. Myrrh was eighteen.

'When I said I had something to tell you,' Myrrh asked her later, 'did you think I was going to say I was pregnant?'

'That would've been better,' her mum replied curtly.

Looking back, she felt relieved that fate had intervened and he unceremoniously dumped her. She had only stayed with him for familiarity and safety, so much like the familiar comfort of her goblin chattering away, telling her she should be grateful for any passing scraps of love.

feed me up
give me more
you owe me
hold out your hands
begging bowl
it will never be enough

CAYENNE

I don't think he knows. Perhaps he does. I can't remember when my ghost lover first appeared, my muse, my confidante. But at night when the moon is waxing or full, I know he'll visit. I am asleep and the sensation of another in bed with us grows. I think my husband must be able to notice as I become aroused by my ghost lover. Even if we have made love in the hours beforehand, it is as if my ghost lover arrives to assert his power in this secret relationship, to dispel the scent of my husband by claiming my body over and over again. When the moon wanes he does not visit me. He is my secret that no one else will discover. How can it be wrong if he is unseen by anyone but me? But he is real to me; I know he's real.

I notice that my husband is more amorous when his daughter has been spending time with him. It seems to excite him, so he acts like a teenager, not attempting to control his bodily urges but exacerbating them so he enters a sort of heightened frenzy. It does not go unnoticed that he is rarely as attentive when we are alone together in the house with no risk of interruption. He repulses me with increasing frequency. Not wanting to be connected in any way to his mucky fantasies, I try to turn a blind eye.

I am scared to leave this place in case my ghost lover does not follow, in case he is tied to this house somehow. He is so real that

I feel he may be the one to impregnate me and not this pathetic mortal man I have been lumbered with.

MYRRH

Myrrh often found her mum in the kitchen when she visited. She was always busy making things, doing things, or writing lists of things to make or do. Her steady influence helped Myrrh feel safe. There was security in knowing her mum's consistency would never waver.

The big kitchen had a walk-in pantry cupboard and separate utility. Pale cream linoleum, painted wood cabinets and stone walls. On the work surface a kettle sat where it had always been stationed, next to the toaster and cooker hob. Shelves had been installed by her dad and now housed jars of spices, packets of loose tea, nuts and other homely ornaments.

A vase in the window had cut flowers a little past their best but still fresh enough to warrant another day's joy. Myrrh noticed they were orange dahlias with a spray of baby's breath. She picked at some fallen petals beside the vase. She didn't like dahlias, their neat showy heads on top of rigid, straight stems. Once, she had sniffed a flower growing proud in the garden, a natural urge to inhale the colour as she would a rose. She'd placed her face up close to the petals and something had caught her eye: a black insect that wriggled free, inches from her nose. It twitched its antennae then disappeared back inside the flower head. Since then, she had shivered at the thought of what those beautiful blooms housed.

Myrrh opened the window and dropped the fallen petals outside then washed her hands in the sink.

'Didn't hear you come in.' Her mum appeared in the doorway holding a yellow duster and spray bottle.

Myrrh always knew she was welcome and didn't need to announce her arrival or pre-book a visit. This was her childhood home, a safe space. Yet he was here too, always with her, wherever she went, even in the safety of her mum's company.

imposter
how dare you
you have what's mine

'Cup of tea?' her mum's voice broke through Goblin's taunts. 'Thought I'd get on with the housework.' Her mum flicked the switch on the kettle. 'Terrible rain last night.'

it's raining, it's pouring
the witch girl is boring
bore a hole in your head
suck out brains
now you're dead

Myrrh listened but her mind was elsewhere. She wanted to be somewhere familiar. Thought it might help rid her of this growing unease. The clock on the wall ticked its usual regular beat. In the fields outside a cow let out a low bellow. As she looked out the window, she could see birds come and go on the seed feeder. In the distance, the wash of grey clouds hung over the low hills.

'Everything okay, love?' Her mum busied herself with the teapot and mugs, fetched milk from the fridge while Myrrh stood by the window.

no love
useless child

'Yeah, I'm feeling a bit, y'know…' Myrrh didn't know how to describe how she felt.

dead

dead and gone
useless
worthless

'Coming down with something?' Her mum furrowed her brow in concern.

down
down into the pit
dead and buried

'Not sure… no, I'm not ill.' Myrrh felt stones pile up on her chest. Why couldn't she say it? Why couldn't she talk about the past, *her* past, with her mum? Her mum was the one who had known her from the start of her life, almost the start.

know yourself
imposter
fake
rip your tongue out
sour milk
mummy's dried up titties

The stones were pressing on her ribcage. It hurt to breathe so she took shallow breaths. She could hear her heartbeat drum inside her ears. The radio seemed too loud. A man's gravelly voice announced the news, grated at the air between her and her mum. She slumped onto a chair and focused on her breathing. *In – out – in – out*, like they did in meditation. Only every time she tried to breathe in, the air felt stuck, the stones piling up inside her, great rocks of grief layered like an ill-balanced wall, precarious and ready to tumble. It could all come crashing down and crush her.

pile it on
layer by layer
bury it

'Biscuit?' Her mum placed a mug of tea on the table in front of her. 'You look a bit peaky.'

peek-a-boo

guess who?
name me

The words were there beneath the stones that Goblin had layered inside her. If only she could muster enough energy to topple the weight and set them free. He wouldn't give up; he never gave up.

weakling
weak little foundling
hold your tongue

It would feel better; she knew it would. If only she could talk about it.

split cream
curdled milk
in your mouth

Outside a tinny rendition of 'Greensleeves' echoed from an ice-cream van.

hold your tongue
rip it out
dunk in blood
mother's milk

'Mum, I'm thinking of—' Myrrh started but the stones were rocks, giant hard-edged rocks ready to crush the breath out of her. She took a sip of her tea at the same time as her mum did, and they both sputtered it back out. She gagged at the foul taste in her mouth, leapt up and stuck her head under the cold water tap, spitting and splashing water onto her tongue.

'Milk's off,' her mum said. 'Sorry love.'

'Greensleeves' chimed out, louder, closer, drowning out the birdsong.

milk's off
milk blood
lap it up
spit it out

Myrrh dried her hands and face on a tea towel, tried to catch her breath. She felt too weak to broach the subject now. Her eyelids felt heavy. She could only think of curling up into a ball under her covers. She needed more strength to tackle this. Goblin was too strong. He thrived on her uncertainty, her hesitancy, planting insecurity in her, layering it over whatever truth was hidden with rough, heavy stones he made her carry.

MYRRH

An elastic feeling tugged at her insides. Was this homing instinct or desperation pulling her apart? It felt ungrounded and dangerous. The unknown was beckoning her to revisit old wounds, to unpick the scabs.

    scab picker
    crusts of blood
    dig your nails in
    rip flesh
    pull out the prize

Myrrh felt sick just contemplating the journey, but she'd bought a ticket and now stood on the platform waiting for the train to Penzance. She wasn't even sure what she'd do when she got there. She'd not planned that far in advance. As though she'd sleepwalked into it, not considering the next steps or the consequences of what she'd start. It had taken all her strength to even muster the courage to get to the station.

    give up
    go home
    lay it to rest

If she were honest, the decision to go felt unripe, too soon to be carefully considered. She wanted to fight against Goblin and his put-downs, but even just trying to ignore his voice was hard.

Her palms were sweaty. Her tongue kept sticking to the roof of her mouth. She looked up at the display to check the train time for the millionth time. It was nearly due. She scrabbled around in her bag for her water bottle but couldn't find it. Damn. She'd left it by the front door when she ran back up to the toilet. Her brain thumped against her skull.

do not go
do not go

A half-opened packet of Fishermen's Friends was the only edible option in her bag. She placed a sweet in her mouth, but it felt odd and furry on her tongue, too soft. She had switched bags in a hurry at the last minute. As well as changing her outfit three times and visiting the toilet more than once, she'd not had much time. She couldn't eat her breakfast either, and now her empty stomach and the thought of travelling for hours made her feel nauseous.

shit it out
madeofshit

The platform was quiet except for a man with a wheeled suitcase and a young woman wearing headphones, scrolling through her phone. Myrrh checked the display again. On time, it read. Expected arrival. Myrrh was an expected arrival once. Awaited and prayed for.

dirty little secret

'You hardly slept those first few weeks,' her mum told her. 'I used to cradle you but you kept your eyes wide open.'

Myrrh wanted to ask her mum about that time, but Goblin had jabbed his spiky fingers down her throat.

cry baby
poor ickle baby
dumped like trash

There were questions she needed to ask her birth mother, too. What were those first moments like after her birth? Why did she decide to give her up? Was she certain who the father was?

Questions that could only be answered by the people who were there at the time, decisions made for her that led her to being where she was today with a whole different set of relatives.

She had no expectations in terms of physical resemblance. Although, fascinated by others' familial features, in her mind's eye she could only muster a human-shaped blur, a void to be filled with texture and colour and a gigantic heavy weight sitting on her chest.

stones
sticks and stones
stones crush bones

A pigeon landed on the opposite platform and strutted to the yellow line near the edge. It pecked at an anonymous crumb and carried on investigating the ground. Myrrh fidgeted with her bag and checked the information board for the millionth time.

forgotten
dead and buried
no one cares

She found an empty bench and sat down, feeling weary and lost, beaten before she had begun her search. What was the point of going? Did she need to go through all this? Wasn't it best to let bygones be bygones?

let it lie
let it die
give it up

More people had turned up on the platform now. Suitcase man was standing ready for the train's arrival, his hand on the upright handle of his case. Myrrh saw the gold band on his ring finger, imagined his family at home kissing him goodbye, waiting for his return. A rush of cold wind channelled past her but she felt hot and sticky, and the band of her jeans felt too tight.

nobody's family
nobody's child

nobody
no body

She thought she might be sick so stood, ready to bolt to the toilet. But it was too late to get there and back if she were to get on the train. The carriages pulled to a stop at the platform, and she inhaled the smoky stench of diesel. All she wanted to do was get home and shut the door.

The man with the suitcase pressed the button to open the train door. Myrrh watched as passengers stepped off and hurried out of the station. No one lingered. Suitcase man lifted his case and disappeared into the carriage. The girl with the headphones had already jumped aboard. The platform was clearing, and Myrrh stood glued to the spot. The whistle sounded somewhere near her, but still she couldn't move. The doors closed. Her head was straining to make the connection. *Move your feet, move your hands.* But her body refused. The train shuddered into motion. Myrrh watched as the train slid away, creeping past her eyes in a blur of dark greys until she was looking at the opposite side of the platform, blinking back tears and abandoning her plans.

MARIAN

Marian put down the mallet and picked up the picture. She positioned the string, tightrope taut against the back of the frame, sliding it to centre on the nail. After shifting it left and right until it was level, she stood back to look. It was a pleasant enough scene: a field with cows and a barn in the foreground filled with hay and the odd abandoned farm implement. It was just something she'd picked up from the charity shop and didn't really need, but its pastoral simplicity made her buy it.

The dogs in the yard were barking, but she ignored them and set about trying to tidy the boxes that seemed to accumulate in the corner of every room. This year she intended on clearing some of the household stuff that seemed to breed when she wasn't looking. She had a sense that something was stirring; it always did this time of year. August was a month invisibly etched on her body in scratchy, loose lines.

She sighed and went to the kitchen, placed her mallet on the worktop and looked out the window at the jasmine in full bloom.

She filled the kettle and put it on to boil then unearthed the book she was reading from underneath a pile of newspapers. A family saga. She had only selected it when she had purchased the painting at the charity shop because it was set in Cornwall, and when she flicked through the pages, she found a hand-written recipe that had been used as a bookmark. *Easy Fruitcake.* She felt obliged to buy the book in order to acquire the recipe but had not got round to making the cake yet.

She poured a glass of water and drank a sip before tipping the rest down the gurgling sink, swilling the glass once more then placing it on the draining board. Abandoning her task of making tea, she returned to her book intent on finishing another chapter before she continued with her chores.

As she settled in her chair to read, the house thrummed and creaked like it was changing gears, ticking and tapping like it had tongues or fingers and was trying to warn her of something. At night she liked to listen out for new sounds, expecting the walls or pipes to offer her a revised tune, but she had been there so long she was as familiar with each rhythmic note as she was with the hymns at church and the way the organist sometimes missed a beat or the choir stumbled on a refrain so it sounded like delayed voices echoing in a cave.

A car passed by slowly on the narrow road at the end of her drive, and its engine stalled. Probably a holidaymaker taking a wrong turn, in need of new directions. Things like satnav didn't work down in the Vale. Some said it was the trees or the dip in the land that prevented the signal, but this was Cornwall, land of the piskies, and Marian had lived here long enough to know they liked to play tricks on the human folk.

She touched the small gold cross hanging from a slender chain on her neck and watched a robin land on the fence post. The visible face of God, that was what the sermon was about last week. It had made no sense at the time, but, like a wave crashing, she realised it did not matter what God looked like. Who knew for sure anyway? She tried to imagine the faces of those who had disappeared from her life, those who had died or become estranged, how quickly those mannerisms seemed to fade or distort with memory.

When it happened all those years ago, she was offered the services of a priest, but it felt too much like the offering of last rites, so she had declined. Therapy wasn't something so freely banded around back in the 1970s, not like now. Now, everyone seemed to have something wrong with them, some mental deficiency that affected their daily life. On reflection, she wished she had spoken up back then about God, about grief, with someone who acted as an intermediary to the spiritual realms. But another faceless helper seemed to only complicate the already complicated process.

It was at that time that she started praying. Like a ritual, each night she'd close her eyes and tightly clasp her hands together to say her prayers, offering them up to God, squeezing her eyes shut and concentrating with earnest. A wing and a prayer, she had heard her friend say, without context, but it had stuck in her mind as the image of an angel spearing up and up into a blue sky, eyes closed, blindly willing itself to safely reach a destination.

Marian put down her book and stared at the boxes. She remembered a few things from that part of her life:
- how he kissed with an urgency that made her breathless;
- limpet shells lined up like mini-pyramids on the doorstep;
- the heat of that hot summer behind her knees and the crook of her elbow in the space where a baby should rest.

MYRRH

Myrrh had always wanted to visit the pyramids in Egypt. It was part of her cultural background, or so she thought. Her putative birth father named on her paperwork: *part-coloured, Egyptian, doctor*. Those scant facts infused her view of a country that she was tentatively linked with. The sheer expanse of time those great structures had endured in the desert, watching over the edge of the city: bizarre, exotic, and reaching for the sky. A treat to herself before she started work at the care home.

Vehicles sounded tinny horns to alert other drivers, bashed-up cars and buses weaved in and out of horse-drawn carts, donkeys and camels plodded amongst the traffic oblivious to the dangers. Mayhem, but with a quaint orderliness, and just beyond the smoke-polluted city centre she was surprised to see, only a stone's throw from the metropolis, those magnificent pyramids and the proud statue of the sphinx. So near to the disarray of modern community life. Up close they appeared even more majestic.

She arrived in the dark on a delayed plane only to discover that the riverboat she had been booked onto had departed without her. No problem, the guide reassured her with servile grace, there would be a taxi. Subtly placed armed guards followed them in a transit van. If she were not with another stranded English couple, she might have felt like she were being kidnapped.

When they did eventually arrive at the boat, two hours later in the dark, they had to walk a plank across the brooding Nile. Their suitcases precariously handed across the divide between the bank and the boat. Hungry and tired, they retreated to their cabins, thankful they had arrived at a resting place regardless of whether it was the correct destination.

The morning greeted Myrrh with roaring engines and churning water as the boat departed at first light to make its way to Luxor. Out of the small window there was the Nile, packed and bustling with rivercraft and people. A sense of nostalgia washed over Myrrh. She felt an affinity to the Egyptians with their polite deference and attentive smiles.

One by one, the passengers caught the dreaded pharaoh's curse and took to their cabins. A holiday to remember. Myrrh missed the trip to the Valley of the Kings. She spent all day alternating between the rancid toilet and the sweat-soaked bed. Camels and hyenas paraded on the ceiling, giant cats with jewels for eyes blinked and purred, crocodiles lumbered towards her, giant-headed cow gods licked her cheeks, jackals snarled into her ears.

Goblin flitted about the room too, chattering like a bird, squatting on his haunches and mimicking her painful bowel movements, and then shrieking with mirth. His bony fingers and pointed face leered at her. The size of a baby but with long, misshapen limbs and ghastly ruched skin all over its lumpy body. She woke to find him crouching on her chest, staring into her face. His sad eyes widened but never blinked. Whenever she woke, he was there watching, grinning into her discomfort.

The fever passed in a few days. The hope that the trip might connect her to the cultural roots she had been denied seemed overambitious as she recovered from the sickness, barely even registering the view. She enjoyed the place but felt cheated as she sat atop the slow-moving boat, dehydrated and empty, watching carefree children run along the riverbank shouting and waving their skinny arms with more energy than she could muster.

Somewhere in this ancient over-populated city, thought Myrrh, *there may be people I am related to*. It was a surreal thought, later reinforced by a waiter at the hotel who asked, 'Where are you from?' as he lingered by their table.

He directed his question at Myrrh, and it was clear he was inquiring about her heritage rather than her nationality. She had a thousand answers to the question, and none. We are not all the same as we are led to believe. Yet we seek similarities in our differences. Some blend into their environment better than others. Myrrh seemed to do this, but her lack of identity gave her no solid foundation. Her goblin reminded her

you don't belong
you don't belong
you don't belong

Once at a train station in France she had stood next to an elderly lady leaning on a stick who chatted nonchalantly to her before departing, not even aware that her smiles and nods hid her lack of linguistic skill. In Greece she was mistaken as a local and met with surprised faces when the German couple (speaking in English) asked her for directions before realising she, too, was a traveller and just as clueless as they were. It was an unexpected attack of racism while travelling in Turkey that left her in no doubt that she had some ethnic signifier about her looks. She had always ticked 'White British' on questionnaires when, in fact, she was not. She didn't know where she had come from.

The waiter returned with more bread.

'I know who it is,' the waiter said, 'You look just like her.'

Myrrh smiled at him, encouraging him to explain.

'I have a friend, a lady doctor, she lives now in Aswan. But from Cairo.'

Myrrh nodded. She hated telling strangers her story but found it seeped out of her before she could stop herself. The meagre information on her adoption paperwork: people latched onto it like she was a sailboat they had permission to board.

'Let me find out the name for you, yes?' His helpfulness a nuisance now. She merely wanted to establish some sort of transient connection to prove that this was the ethnic group she belonged to or came from. Not an in-depth search to trace what would just be another person who someone else thought she looked like. She found it trivial, insensitive even.

Myrrh hoped he was only making conversation, that he'd forget by the morning. She could not bear another mealtime with a stranger performing some sort of mock ancestry search.

The following day he was not there and instead their waiter was a smaller, slighter man with a more austere expression and professional distance. Myrrh was thankful for this. Talking about where she came from exhausted and embarrassed her at the same time, and she couldn't help but think her goblin was being eerily silent on the matter.

SANDRA

Sandra peeled off her marigolds and hung them neatly on the draining rack while looking out the window at the privet hedge. He'd been out there again that morning before he went to work, trimming it like he would the hairs on his chest and inside his ears. She worried what would happen when he finally retired, whether he would be one of those men who suddenly expired, as if all his allocated time on earth had been used up at work, a machine going kaput. The thought did not sadden her but instead gave her a momentary feeling of elation, as though his death would offer her a reprieve of sorts.

She pulled the tight clip from the back of her head and let her dyed blonde hair fall loose. A shiver ran down her back, a touch on that sensitive part of her neck that he seemed to ignore when, and if, he kissed her. Now he only ever gave her a quick peck on the cheek to say goodbye: a habit like tying his shoelaces or brushing his teeth. When had the weather of their romance turned dull and overcast? Why had they been blindly groping their way through what nearly didn't start in the first place?

She picked up the tub of birdseed and went to slip on her shoes, paused, then walked barefoot outside into the garden. The shrubs and plants pulsed around her in vivid patterns, the roses he so tenderly clipped looked pert and showy, and the magnolia showered petals on the neat lawn and seemed to mock her in their naked beauty. *Furry rabbit's ears*, she thought, as she took one in her palm and stroked it against her cheek. She placed the tub of birdseed on the garden seat and unwrapped her cardigan. *Look at us*, the plants seemed to say, *He loves us as we are. He touches us all the time. He touches us like he touches all those other women.*

It was not a hot day, but the sun was shining and a cool breeze made the hairs lift on her bare arms. She slipped her blouse up over her head and quickly stepped out of her skirt, feeling momentarily foolish at standing outside in her underwear. She unhooked her bra, easily shaking it loose down over her arms. Then, sliding her underwear down over her thighs, she flung them at the hedge, letting out a small groan of effort. They landed like a spent streamer on the neatly ordered leaves. She stood for a moment with her hands held on her hips and her face heavenward. Then, without hesitation, she roared like a lioness. The sound echoed from her core, and, after it had exited her body, she squatted down so her haunches were almost touching the dewy grass and her toes and fingers were pressing into the lawn. This was the most alive she had felt in years. She breathed in and out, inhaling the scent of grass and soil.

She remembered the midwife from when she was in labour with her first son, trying to coax her from the floor of the hospital where she was positioned on all fours, hair hanging around her face in wet strings, the soft tutting of disapproval and spiky fingers on her shoulder urging her to lie back on the bed. *Sweetheart*, the woman had called her, much to her distaste. She had sensed that the midwife was as embarrassed by her animal pose and swaying breasts as by the noises that came from deep within her. This is birth, she had reasoned. It is not meant to be pretty, or contained, or directed. It was the only part of her life she felt any control over, and what right had those strangers telling her what to do, how to behave.

Her husband was predictably absent, working, ironically, as a gynaecologist, tending to other women's needs. He missed the crowning of his first son's head, arriving after she had been arranged neatly and cleanly in the hospital bed with their firstborn in her arms.

She lifted herself from those old memories and stood awkwardly, not used to crouching down for so long. As she turned, she saw her husband standing by the patio doors regarding her as he would an unidentified bug on one of his roses. Although he had seen her naked, touched her body intimately, this setting was unfamiliar territory. They had never made love in the garden, nor any other part of the house except the bedroom where he insisted she wore some layer of clothing over her bare skin. Perhaps it was something to do with the clinical aspect of his work examining women. He could not bear to look upon her skin with the eye of a lover. Yet, from her viewpoint, when covered, she felt more like his patient this way. Once, she had tried to encourage him to be more romantic by setting out soft cushions on the floor of the lounge by the open fire, but he had just picked them up, and neatly tucked them back into the corners of the sofa, tutting at her foolishness and frivolity.

'I forgot my phone,' he said, as if to himself, and went back into the house, ignoring her nakedness, ignoring her altogether.

She retrieved her underwear from the laurel bush and stooped to collect her fallen clothing. It was not worth trying to explain, and he didn't demand an explanation anyway. She was not unintelligent; she had a degree in linguistics and was adept at most subjects if she applied herself. He would not have understood the complexities of emotion even if she had drawn diagrams or written it in one of those medical journals he studied so carefully: *Here is the heart* (she imagined herself sketching a sleek arrow towards the ventricles and atria). *This is where love is rumoured to reside.*

She heard the front door close behind him as she awkwardly wriggled back into her skirt. The label irritated the small of her back, so she looped her finger through it. How easy must it be for him to cut through living flesh with his scalpel, to reach those parts that needed intervention? She saw how he carefully snipped the roses with sharpened secateurs, letting the dead stalks fall. He would pick up each dead part and deposit it on the compost heap so the lawn was always spotless. Even the chaos of nature was contained in their neat back garden.

When she had suggested they get a puppy or a rescue dog, his first response had alluded to the mess it would leave, the time and energy in looking after it: hair on the furniture, muddy footprints on the carpets, faeces on the grass that even when scooped up would leave an unsightly residue, walks and feeding, trips to the vet. And what if they wanted to go away on vacation or visit her mother at short notice? He had a point. But she still resented the fact that he reasoned it away, logically laying out why that option was not appropriate for them. The choice was taken from her.

I'm going to tear off each layer of my body, she thought, *starting with my hair.* She imagined follicles ripped from her scalp, complete with flakes of dead cells, then the skin on her face and jaw, and all those sinewy parts, her muscles and tendons flayed like slow-boiled meat. *All the parts that retained memory*, she thought, *peeled away and discarded without care. Remember, remember the pink of September. She wanted red. Bright, gushing vermillion like blood from an arterial vein. September, the month it all imploded.*

A butterfly landed on the windowsill and flexed its wings up and down, catching the sunlight. It seemed scorched as if the air had dehydrated its delicate shape. Its wings were deformed like a slice of dried beetroot. She stared at it for a moment before it tried to lift its body, and she watched, horrified, as it plummeted to the ground and lay on the patio slab, two redundant wings opening and closing, slowly applauding the end of its life.

She felt compelled to pick it up, but in the back of her mind a warning flashed up reminding her of the delicacy of butterfly wings, coated with waterproof dust, the slightest touch able to destroy the equilibrium. Her phone buzzed, jolting her from this train of thought just as the letterbox rattled; a singular smack of paper on the floor tiles announced the simultaneous arrival of news.

She picked up her phone and saw a text from her son:

> Are you free for a quick chat I need to talk
> about something. It's private. I've kept it to
> myself but need to see what you think x

Her mind raked over the word: 'private'. Privacy and secrecy seemed complicit. And her firstborn son was never one to text about trivia. He was always sincere even when using social media. No words or phrases were wasted. Yet, as a mother, Sandra sensed his urgency to unburden whatever was loaded on him.

She put her phone down on the table, went to the utility sink, put her rubber gloves back on and sprayed the already clean basin, and then scrubbed it with the scouring pad. The running of cold water, the rinsing of soapy suds, the removal of her rubber gloves, and the neat placement of them over the mixer tap were all carried out in silence. She craved cigarettes as she stared at the ceramic sink that shined so bright it became a milky mirror.

Sandra picked up her phone from the table and read the text again. Then dialled her son's number.

CAYENNE

Cooking programmes heal my innards. It's the act of watching alchemy in its entirety from conception to fruition. Placing ingredients in a pan, adding heat, mixing with the other parts of the dish allows a moment of reflection. An analogy of love. You would not ingest it at this stage. It would taste raw, undigestible, unpleasant. Yet, time, the stirring, change of temperature, the shaking and attention, leads to tenderly gathering disparate parts in one place. Textured, softness beneath. Layers all adding to the complexity of how it will be received.

I'm watching an American woman bake an intensely chocolatey cake and she keeps saying *bittersweet*. The sun has been beating down all day, and all I have eaten is a square of dark chocolate. I try to drag myself from the sofa, but I only get as far as putting one foot on the floor. Dark, brown sludge tips into the cake tin as if an unformed creature were trying to escape its fate.

Measure this. Stir this. Add this slowly. She makes it look easy. Layering over the mess in my head. A stiff peak of cream makes me salivate. Soft pureed fruit drips from a spoon. Delicately placed pink eyeballs glisten on top of the cream, still moist from the cavity they have been plucked from. They blink back at me.

I vomit into my hands.

SANDRA

'How long have you known?' Sandra asked him over the phone.

'I received a message last month. I didn't want to... you know... I didn't know... could it be true?'

She swallowed. This was not how she imagined it. *One day*, she thought. One day she might discover some secret about her husband. An allegation of sexual abuse by a colleague or a patient. Thinking it most likely to involve infidelity, this could be the tipping point that proved her suspicions all these years. A whole other family existing in a town she had not even heard of? But the involvement of her son was too much; the way her husband's actions were now infiltrating their children's lives was her worst nightmare. Her two sons had always been her sanctuary, her reason for enduring his undesirable traits. When she met her husband, he had been coated in syrupy words: gentleman, well-mannered, smooth, chivalrous. Where there was once pride at his attentiveness to her, anger now welled up inside her when she imagined his hand on the small of another woman's back, his fingernails gently pressing beneath hers, or that enigmatic smile he brought out on occasions to instantly charm those in his company.

'How did she trace you?'

'Online. I guess she knew our name – Dad's name.'

'What did she say?'

'Just wanted to find out. That sort of thing. Listen, Mum, you know how hard it is to talk to him about the past… I mean, do you think it's true?'

'Why did she contact you? Why not write to *him*?'

'I know as much as you. She said she sent a letter to his clinic. Didn't get a reply.'

His phone was crackling in and out of signal until the words were like ash scattered in the breeze and his voice took on a robotic rhyme of half-syllables and staccato notes.

'Shit,' she said, and again, 'Shit!'

She heard the beeps of the phone line expiring, and the image of her son's face disappeared from the screen. Inside the waistband of her skirt, the label continued to irritate her skin. With one sharp tug, she tried to rip it out, but the seam held strong and remained attached like a creature clinging on for dear life. She swore again and walked towards the snug where she kept her sewing kit.

It was happening. Secrets were being unearthed, but not in the way she had anticipated. Her own secrets would have to remain buried for now. She needed to find out once and for all what happened all those years ago.

She rummaged in her sewing basket for a pair of scissors to deal with the scratching label, and her finger met with a sharp stab. A loose needle had pierced her skin and a small dot of blood oozed to the surface. She sucked at her finger, letting the metallic tang seep onto her tongue just as she remembered a time, shortly before they married, when she had received another message.

Back then it was a letter from a stranger.

MYRRH

Myrrh had agonised over the words to put in her email to him. It had overshadowed her enjoyment of the holidays. Instead of relaxing and watching reruns of Christmas movies, she had carefully written and rewritten the message, trying not to sound overeager or too hostile. She wanted him to reply after all. He had been named as her father. It was a big piece of information. Her birth mother had put his name on her birth certificate. Those scraps of paper she had found in the tin held such weight now that she was fitting the pieces together. The anticipation was suffocating her. Each time she refreshed her inbox she felt the heavy thud of palpitations in her chest. Until, finally, his reply. She took a deep breath and clicked on it.

One does not miss what one never had.

But what if one knows what might be missing?

But what if one knows what one never had and it wasn't their choice?

But what if one does miss it?

But, but, but, but…

loser

fucking freak

no one misses you

It had taken her days to compose her initial letter exactly as she had wanted, but barely any time at all to find the man named on her birth certificate as her father online. The name, his age and job: it all lined up. She caught herself staring at his picture, finding similarities between the two of them. When she clicked *Send* on the email, after all that time agonising over it, she felt sick. She was unearthing secrets long buried, secrets that his family probably knew nothing about.

All those hours she had given over to thinking about him seemed wasteful now as she read the long-awaited reply. Scattered phrases like seeds on barren ground, those words had no more substance than his existence. He was just another person, alive on the Earth, who viewed their past actions as a distant continent: out of sight, out of mind.

'Dear Miss…' it began, already formal in tone. *'I am writing to clarify issues you raised with my son as well as a letter you sent to my clinic…'*

Could she read tension in those spaces? The message was spattered with his memories, some hazy, others startlingly specific: *'to my surprise, she referred to me as her boyfriend!!'* Those exclamation marks seemed cruel, condescending in tone.

Myrrh touched her computer keys to let the words flick back on the screen then clicked the small x in the corner to shut it off. As she looked out the window, she stared into the middle distance, not even seeing the blue sky or the soft focus of heat lifting from the ash trees on the hills. Something in her body sagged.

For years while growing up she had boasted her ethnicity as if it were a totem of power. At first, she wore it proudly as a badge, much like the ones she had acquired as a Guide. Later, as she grew older and met more diverse groups of people than her small town had nurtured, it became apparent that she never really *owned* her heritage or nationality. She was unplaced so deflected the inquisitions of others and never showed her unease.

'Where are you from?' she was asked tentatively after initial introductions were out of the way. What they were really asking was, *Who are your parents? What is your heritage?* And to ask an adopted person that question is paramount to showing an addict the drug of their choice. It leads to inevitable wallowing in self-analysis, followed by self-loathing, followed by more questioning, followed by guilt, followed by shame, followed by (in Myrrh's case) chocolate.

Responses got stuck in her throat. 'I'm from–' she would cheerily state, which led to blank looks, and in order to avoid embarrassment (theirs not hers) she started apologising for not knowing the full story of her parentage, she had been a bad baby, and therefore it was her fault. 'Long story,' she'd mutter, laughing light-heartedly, while her guts churned with shame and the goblin gnawed on her.

bad baby
who wants a bad baby
loser

She played a dangerous game with men, toying with them as a cat would a snake, but exercising caution in case she had to commit herself to any sort of deep affection. A string of unsuitable relationships flicked across the screenplay of her mind. They all seemed to satisfy her need for attention at the time, but were never the 'right' ones. Her absent, faceless father held the position of power, and he had not earned any scrap of respect from her.

His role, to date, held the unsavoury job title of 'sperm donor'. A role he still denied some decades after the event. And his flaky recollection of dates seemed even more strikingly suspicious. Unless he was recalling another woman that he had got pregnant. It was distinctly possible.

The odds were not in his favour. She had invested time in finding out who he was. Not to mention his name written boldly, in a dated typewriter font, on her birth certificate. Not to mention the only living person able to corroborate the fact, her birth mother, had put his name on that official piece of paper knowing that someday it might be read.

She flicked back to the list of emails and opened the one she had just closed:

'...*It would not make sense to base your belief that I am your father solely on a name on a piece of paper.*' But what else could she base it on? Was it all a lie? A cover story for the real truth? Maybe these named people really were unrelated strangers, and her real parents were kept secret to protect her from the truth? No matter how difficult the process, she would find out even if it hurt.

The goblin shrieked

no one wants you
shrivelled up old hag
barren bitch

Myrrh curled up in a ball on her bed and closed her eyes. She tossed and turned in every direction, but still the knot of grief tightened around her throat, threatening to choke her. Goblin's taunts were present right up until the moment sleep claimed her tired body.

too bitter and too old to be someone's baby now

CAYENNE

A tight fist of anxiety, clenching and unclenching in my stomach, each time there is a family gathering. Or even just a meal arranged by her and announced several hours before the occasion. In reality, it is not so much her outward behaviour as the buoyant manipulation of her father. It is impossible to imagine she will ever break out and lead her own life. She enthuses each gathering with her own agenda. Although she is not the brightest mind in the world, she is certainly the most adept at getting her own way: chattering about horses, hunting, horses and horses.

She talks only to her father, rarely communicates with me. Her snidey remarks in front of others results in even more palpable tension. Now the crumbling relationship is even more derelict, bricks crashing down onto foundations that were already rocky, windowpanes shattered. I cannot wait for sleep to take me away from these monsters, back to my ghost lover who understands my every need.

The anxiety has always been there, but it's heightened when I feel outnumbered. I tried to ignore the sickly exchanges between her and her father. Her sullen moods, the way she slams down of bags and coats and keys onto freshly wiped surfaces. She digs her fake nails into his Achilles heel; she is his only remaining blood relative.

MYRRH

Maybe it was the back-handed snipes about my hair, or clothes, or body shape. Maybe it was the… I can't say the word. Maybe it was because she was young and fertile and fecund and ripe and blooming and how easily she would find the route to motherhood as if it were her God-given right like everything else she did not have to fight for.

I think I hate her!

MARIAN

In his garments the vicar looked like he'd just got out of bed. A blue cassock with creased white cotton and an almost stereotypical gaze as if heaven were just about within his grasp.

The world is going to end in precisely three minutes. The world is going to end in precisely...

A countdown started in Marian's head, and there was absolutely nothing she could do but run through all the things she should have done in the infinite time she seemed to have had before the apocalypse had been dumped on her, without notice, like a catastrophic meteor.

Fires rapidly spreading, smoke rising up, bomb blasts, dust blocking the sun, the smell of singed hair, bodies littering the streets...

You can pack a lot of thoughts into a brain in less than three minutes. Her final thoughts rattled through her head:

- People she loved.
- People she should have tried harder to keep in touch with.
- People she should have met but didn't because she never believed time would run out.
- Not finishing her nursing course.
- Things she could have learned: Spanish, playing the piano, surfing.
- What did the Sistine Chapel smell like?

- The baby.
- The pain, the scars, the healing.

Marian breathed deeply, trying to remind herself that it was just her brain confusing her, a momentary blip. This was not the end of the world, just a surge of hormones, a chemical response to her body changing.

An audience with God. A prayer. A conversation. Those were the only words spoken by the vicar that hung in the air above her and offered no respite at all. The truth was, the world wasn't ending, and she would have to carry on. What else could she do?

CAYENNE

Things have become worse between us. He regularly states that I'm in a mood and he can't live with it. Blame is placed squarely on me like he is keeping score in a one-sided match. Even my attempt to rectify any terse situation is met with indifference. He says I'm in a mood because I'm jealous when he gets on with his daughter. It all revolves around his 'daughter' and heaven forbid I forget that they are related. Every time we are in the room together, she mentions something that her father did with her mother, how her mum used to do this and, 'Didn't you and Mum like dancing together?' or 'That was Mum's favourite flower', and 'Didn't Mum used to make this home look welcoming?'

Then there are the sideways knocks at me: 'It looks like an old people's home in here,' or 'Get rid of that old teapot, it looks old-fashioned,' or 'I think you need to clean this up.' Or 'That chair looks rank you need to give me a lift you need to stop washing my clothes like that you need to be here at this time why don't you ever smile what is wrong with you what time is supper,' and on and on and on.

When we argued last night, he accused me of being pissy because I can't stand him getting on and having fun with his daughter. I am only boiling over at the jibes that have slapped me so frequently across my face. He openly states how he has fun with her. It feels like he is saying she doesn't have fun with me around. It feels like he's saying I'm only fun when we have sex. It feels like he's saying I'm not the centre of attention. Our physical relationship is on and off like a kettle, and, although he says he has never been as close to anyone – or as open with anyone or as in love with anyone – I doubt what he is saying; and of course he will never prove this as I don't know anything about his previous relationships.

He uses sex as a means of communication, a reward system to reassure me I am wanted. But I no longer need this. I have my ghost lover. I slip beneath the covers and detach my thoughts from this life. This is time for me and my ghost lover, the only one I can rely upon.

MYRRH

August in Cornwall does not guarantee sunshine, and the year Myrrh decided to find her birth mother had claimed the wettest June on record, a washout for festivals and outdoor events. Myrrh felt she had been spying, snooping around by typing the address she had found on her adoption paperwork into Google Maps, rotating the camera to see if she could catch blurred images of people. Trees obscured the house, fully in leaf, and a narrow road with no road markings led to another property more fully in view. She scoured the photograph: a five-barred wooden gate in need of repair, weather worn with green moss; weeds growing upwards in the gravelled driveway in random bursts; an old blue Escort parked, number-plate blotched out; and a dog, mouth open in mid-bark at the passing photographer.

When she arrived, it was much as she had viewed it on the computer. The same gate, weeds in the gravel. But there were no people to welcome her. It was like a ghostly glen, a mirage. She killed the engine and sat for a while thinking what to do next. She thought about marching up to the door but could hear a dog barking, so stayed outside the gate. A thousand questions ran through her head. Why had she come so ill-prepared? Could any preparation be useful for such a meeting? If there was no one home, then what was the use of waiting? Was it possible to sense, like a wolf or a lamb, someone you were related to? Would it be instant recognition?

She drove away from the deserted cottage and found a café nearby. She ordered a coffee and was suddenly joined by a woman who asked, 'On holiday?'

'Sort of, just visiting relatives.' Not a total lie but not the whole truth either.

lies, all lies

no one wants you

'Where are you heading tonight?

'Home.' Myrrh sipped her drink and admired this stranger's calm demeanour. Even so, her deft questions felt like an interrogation.

failure

useless bad baby

The lack of connection she felt for her unmet relatives was like a dull ache in her abdomen. Her disappointment and low mood in not being able to feel a bond or sense of connection flavoured the whole visit, complementing the dull weather.

'I'm a street pastor,' the woman explained; her previous night had been spent parading the streets of Truro tending to the needs of the drunk and emotionally disjointed. She explained how she handed out cheap flip-flops to girls who insisted on wearing uncomfortable but fashionable footwear that pinched and blistered their feet. By the end of the night, they'd be stumbling barefoot on pavements clutching their high heels by the straps.

'I listen to their stories, the rambling mess of their subconscious surfacing, the loose tongues of the intoxicated.' These lost souls purged themselves after they had gone through the initiation of preparing their clothes, applying makeup, and scenting their bodies. After the inevitable decline of the night there were some who were left abandoned by friends. The *unlucky* loners wandered into her care, perhaps clueless to their vulnerability.

abandoned

unlucky

lost

'Are you local?' Myrrh asked, to be polite.

'Yes, I've been street pastoring for twenty years, holding back the hair of vomiting youngsters. Not sure much has changed in all that time.'

nothing changes

no one cares

The woman reflected on this. Nowadays everything seemed so immediate, news travelling faster than ever.

'Everyone wants to be heard,' she said and politely sipped her coffee, looking into Myrrh's face as if recognising something untapped.

pah!

loser

The woman was so full of belief, Myrrh felt incapable of revealing who she was, as if she were a fraud to own her identity. The goblin screamed

traitor, traitor

why don't you tell her who you really are?

why don't you tell her about the mess inside of you?

'There is always a reason why people behave a certain way,' the woman told her. 'No one is immune from consequences or totally oblivious to the effect of their own actions.'

chop it out

carve it up

burn it

Myrrh wanted to debate this statement. It seemed her birth parents had little forethought before creating her. She was more than certain that they had not planned to procreate when they had briefly met all those years ago.

It was a mistake.

She was a mistake.

She wanted to divulge all the personal details about her life to this stranger: the wasted journey and how she had not planned to drive to the address printed on her adoption paperwork but found herself sitting outside a stranger's house not knowing what to do. How she had felt as a child, the loneliness, the guilt at wanting something more than the circumstances life had dealt her. The feeling that, always, there was something missing twinned with the guilt of having to feel grateful she had been chosen.

lies, all lies

bad baby

stained from birth

But Myrrh never really revealed anything. All she did was talk about the weather, the traffic, the trivial details of her journey. Goblin flexed his bony fingers and dug them into her spleen. The woman nodded and sipped her tea, allowing Myrrh to chatter on.

Myrrh made her way to the counter to pay for coffee, offering to buy the woman's drink. The gesture was greeted with more gratitude and a brief, awkward hug from the woman, who waited until the transaction had taken place. Myrrh felt obliged to leave with her when in fact she needed to go to the toilet. This ridiculous need to please people extended as far as neglecting her own nagging bladder. She watched the woman reverse out of her car-parking space. Only then did Myrrh re-enter the coffee shop and relieve herself, realising that she had not asked the woman's name and had quite forgotten her face already.

CAYENNE

Here, in silence, no need to respond, to react, just breathe in and breathe out. I feel it in my stomach, my heart, my womb.

I know I am meant to be a mother because all around me this world blooms and grows and I will too, whatever that takes. Roses climb up over the window frames, and strong vines furl over the fence. I hear the strong current of the river wash the dark sediment downstream.

I transfer my energies to my ghost lover. He has rescued me from myself, it seems, this creature who knows me better than I know myself. I'm laid bare on my bed each night, and he delves inside me as if a sharp knife is slicing all the badness away.

It feels real so it must be.

Although, when I wake, I find my head heavy on the pillow and my shoulders tense when I realise I am back in this loveless house.

'Do you love me?' I ask my husband.

'I don't know,' he replies.

MYRRH

To have come all that way and not to have made any progress was
disheartening. Myrrh had imagined her birth mother opening the
door, the first glimpse of each other, and a welcoming of sorts.
The talk with a stranger in a coffee shop had goaded her to try
again. She had made the first steps in her journey: wasn't she
entitled to know where she came from, who she came from?

She pulled up outside the house again and got out of the
car. But she couldn't bring herself to ring the doorbell, and the
sound of a dog repeatedly barking probably signified that no one
was home.

She sneaked around to the back gate that was unlatched and
pushed it, making sure the dog could not reach her if it was indeed
running free and not contained in the building. It might've been
friendly but she was, after all, a stranger trespassing.

She peered through the window from a distance at first then
stepped onto the soil of the flower bed, shading her eyes so she
could get a better look in.

The kitchen looked dated: melamine units and tired furniture.
A few plates with a smattering of cutlery stacked by the sink, a pile
of newspapers on the table, and cardboard boxes stacked against
one wall. The inner door was shut and must have led to another
room where the dog now barked insistently.

It could probably smell that she didn't belong.

Myrrh returned to the front of the house, and, as she came through the gate, the door to the neighbour's house opened wide as if the neighbour had been biding his time, waiting for her to pass by.

'Can I help you?' A man, probably late into his retirement, regarded her with amiable suspicion.

'I'm looking for someone,' Myrrh replied.

'Anyone in particular?' He stepped out into the light and pulled the door closed behind him. He looked frail and tired, and his hand rested heavily on the door frame.

'I'm not even sure I've got the right house,' Myrrh blurted out. The neighbour looked at her even more warily.

'I can leave a message if you like.' He sounded friendly but she couldn't read his blank face. 'I'm here most of the time.'

Myrrh thanked him but quickly made her way back to her car, not even daring to look behind. He would only be watching her. *Here most of the time.* She had no doubt he would be phoning up the neighbourhood watch after he had scribbled her number plate.

Typical, she thought, *showing up like that unannounced.* She had psyched herself up expecting only one outcome, not prepared for there to be no one to greet her. The sky was threatening rain, and a sudden gust alerted her to the change in weather, making her look up into the trees. They seemed to move in unison, to be connected even though their branches grew apart. She thought of tangled roots slipping down deep below the surface, the unseen parts. And the unlikely scenario that her roots could ever truly be discovered. What if she never found the answers? What if she lived her life forever searching for something that could never be unearthed? What if she was never meant to know the truth? What if the goblin was right?

lies, all lies

She shivered as the first drops of rain started falling.

CAYENNE

Numerous attempts last night to get him to react and make up with me were met with complacency. I kissed his shoulder and said 'goodnight', thinking he might reciprocate or turn and embrace me. He didn't. After I turned out the light, I asked him again what was wrong and he spat the words back at me, 'Nothing is wrong.' He's lying. I asked him again. He said, 'It's you,' and, 'You've been in a mood all day because I had fun with my daughter for ten minutes this morning'. And then he goes on to say he spends much more time with me and he wants to spend the rest of his life with me and she will not be under our feet forever but she is young and needs to learn.

All this emphasis on time. I tell him it's not about time, it's about her chipping remarks, it's about her manipulative behaviour, it's about the fact he wants to be a father to her but not to my child, our child, and I'm playing a losing game here. Doomed to be a silent wallflower that has no right but to witness the solid weight of another family connection.

I retreat downstairs until midnight and he doesn't come down to reconcile. I go back up to bed and he says he needs to go to sleep, so I go in the spare room and, when I've done this before, he's come in and said in a gentle voice, 'Come on, Princess. I don't want to sleep on my own.' But this time he stays where he is and does nothing. I listen as he gets up to have a piss then goes back to bed. I enter the bedroom and watch the rise and fall of the sheets as he snores then lope back to the spare room, back and forth three times, until eventually I think I will pass out through tiredness.

I wake at 5.30am. It is just as well because he had turned the alarm off, knowing I need to catch an early train. It is easy to hate him. But I need to endure this for a while longer.

MYRRH

'Snakes,' Enid whispered in a more lucid moment, 'are a very forgiving species. They are persecuted by man because they don't have voices.' Myrrh watched her as she spoke, eyes fixed like steel. 'Sometimes the strongest creature doesn't need to make a sound.' Goblin was always chattering away; maybe he wasn't as strong as she gave him credit for.

Enid was one of her favourites at the nursing home. She was nearly one hundred but had the tenacity of a teenager, and her wild flights of fancy provided superficial entertainment. She had deteriorated quite significantly in the few years Myrrh had known her, but Myrrh could sense a strength within that kept her spirit circumnavigating her disintegrating body.

When she started working there, the residents became another family group to compartmentalise. The sadness crept up on her sometimes when she thought about how old and frail they were. Yet each one had a story, a life lived somewhere beyond the limited spaces of the home and the town. *They were young once*, she thought, *with their own rich history of connections, someone's daughter, someone's son*.

When she was a teenager Myrrh went through a phase of studying the facial features of strangers, trying to pick out a resemblance with her own. She used to think they had eyes like hers, or similar cheeks, even the same placement of dimples on their chin. The worst kind of reminder that she resembled no one in her family was when she spent time with them. She could see the quirky trademark slant in noses of aunties and nieces, the unmistakable faces of siblings, fathers and sons. Even distant cousins within the family seemed to fit together.

She drew faces on almost everything: notepads and exercise books, old receipts, her books, her diary, lining out the profiles or the creases found at the corner of mouths. She was the odd one out in a game of *Happy Families* trying to slot in. She was like a butterfly alighting on a flower, gathering what it needs before moving on. Her soul never felt settled so it continued searching, yearning, trying to find its place. One way of satiating that need was by creating new families to fill the void.

Families can take all kinds of guises, some supportive and healthy, others destructive or stifling. Throughout her adolescence, she joined many groups, large and small, insular and diverse. She sought out those with similar interests or habits to combat the loneliness and need for acceptance; Brownies, Girl Scouts, youth groups, drama groups, Chess Club, book clubs, art groups, religious groups, friends from school, friends from other schools, friends from work, people she met on her travels, people she met at parties, friends of friends, friends of friends of friends. The groups were as transient as her displacement; some remained a part of her life but mostly she moved on or they moved on or she cut them out.

Myrrh remembered Alice in the corner shop when she was growing up, and how she used to shoot a look if kids were being too rowdy, especially if there were other customers. The ferocity of her stare needed no explanation and nearly always had the desired disciplinary effect. She leaned forward on the counter between the till and the display of tinned meat, palms flat and shoulders arched back. Her lips were pursed, and the red lipstick made them seem like she'd just finished drinking the blood of her last victim. Her eyes would peer over the top of her glasses. Robbie mentioned once that he thought she was a vampire because her long fingernails grazed his wrist when she handed him his change.

But Myrrh could sense Alice's softness with an acute intuition, a sort of superpower at discerning others' motivations that lay beneath the surface. What she liked about Alice was her ability to be herself. She didn't seem to fit in with any of the other groups in the village, yet she always turned up, took part. She seemed comfortable being herself, which was something Myrrh found tough.

Alice had not been born in the area so was not related to anyone nearby, and she had no children and as far anyone knew; she had never married either (she was known as Miss Eyre to most). Alice seemed to know who she was and what she stood for, even with the clucking of the other women or some unverified gossip that was doing the rounds. Myrrh found comfort in her silent integrity.

But the silence she couldn't handle was from the two people she wanted to make a sound. The house in Cornwall refused her. The email she received back from *him* was dismissive. She was finally ready to meet them, to get answers to all her questions, and all she got back was nothing. Goblin stirred. Why had her birth mother chosen to ignore her? Why had her birth father denied her very existence? Hadn't she waited long enough?

MARIAN

Marian knew at the time he would never accept paternity. She was shocked into the action of requesting his medical history by the social worker. *We will write to him*, they said. *It's important to have the father's records on file*, they said. *It's important to know as much as possible about both parents*, they said. *For the baby*, they said. She felt embarrassed to ask him for any involvement when they hardly knew each other. The decision to give the child away when it was born wracked her with guilt. She didn't know if she could go through with it.

Even more mortifying was that she had to get other uninvolved people to sign the release papers. Spilling her secret to those she wished never knew. What had they to do with the *circumstance* she had gotten herself into? As if the birth did not provide enough shame and humiliation to harbour, she then had to ask the father of this unexpected baby for his medical records. *For the baby's file*, they said.

Names and dates and dotted lines all playing their part like contour lines on a map showing how steep the ground rises, where the boundaries lay or who claimed ownership, and history layered upon itself like clods of earth laid over a coffin.

CAYENNE

I hear muttering in the kitchen below, the soft growl of his voice and a higher-pitched, clipped tone. Why are they up so early? I don't want him to reveal to her that we are having a bad time. The voices rise to a crescendo. The front door squeaks open then crashes shut. The echo of the slamming door makes it seem louder. She has not greeted me once in the past few weeks, and when I did attempt to engage in conversation – a friendly, jaunty note I left asking if she'd had a good day – it resulted in a flat retort almost straight away criticising my unhip way of leaving notes.

Why do I bother with her at all?

Mid-morning and the relationship between us continues to be as fragile as glass. We are tentative, like poker players unsure of showing our hands. He is quiet and subdued as I leave to put some things in my car, but I realise I have forgotten something. As I re-enter the kitchen I find him wiping tears from his eyes.

We hug each other and kiss and cry. The game continues.

'Do you know what she's doing?'

'I don't think she is clever enough to do that.'

'I know I'm not her mother.'

'No.'

'Do you not see how she treats me?'

'She's young.'

'Old enough to know better.
'She's my daughter.'
'*She's my daughter.*' I try to mimic his whiny response but my mouth fills with vomit.

MYRRH

'Green cars are bad luck.' Her mum held some superstitions. Robbie's car had a little bit of rust above the wheel arches that had been painted over, mushrooming like a misshapen fruit. Myrrh just thought the colour of your car was supposed to say something about your personality: trends, she supposed, like clothes or handbags, along with the make or model. Robbie had a bright green Ford Capri.

He wore thick-rimmed glasses and had had his ears pinned back when he was seven. He got his braces stuck on the iron railings outside school when George Ford dared him to bite through one for half of his Toblerone. But he never got angry; he was the kindest, most generous boy she had ever met. If they rooted about on his parent's compost heap for treasure and he found an old lump of metal or a smooth triangle of porcelain, he'd give it to her because he knew how she liked to collect random objects. He needed an inhaler just to run and catch the bus, all wheezy with bits of white spit coming out the corner of his mouth. But his was the first mouth she ever kissed. And she would forever remember that.

On her seventeenth birthday Robbie said as a present she could drive his precious green Capri, round the back lanes if she fancied it. They could go to the disused airfield where there was more space and it was sort of legal.

He drove out to a quiet spot on a long straight drove between the fields, his Capri like a neon highlighter on the moor. The roads were set among the ditches in a crosshatch pattern running to the higher ground of the Angus Ridge that followed the Roman road to Glastonbury. Once, all the land would have been mile upon mile of marshland, flooded for most of the year. The sea would have met the lowlands and rivers, and boats would have sailed towards the Tor standing like a giant beacon to weary travellers.

'Move the seat so your feet can reach the pedals.'

'Mirror, Signal, Manoeuvre,' she repeated like a mantra, looking in the rear-view mirror and seeing a long stretch of fields behind them.

'You'll wanna turn the engine on first,' Robbie said, laughing and pointing to the bunch of keys still dangling from the ignition. She turned the key too far and it let out a squealing retch as the engine pumped to life.

'Just get a feel for the clutch now.' He was deadly serious but she still couldn't help sniggering. She felt she was playing at being a grown-up. 'Press your foot down on the left pedal and you'll see how much pressure you need.' She did as he said, listening to the engine hum.

'Now put it into first gear. Keep your foot down on the clutch pedal.' She gripped the steering wheel with her right hand, not wanting to let go. Then she pushed the gearstick forward with her left and sat waiting for the next instruction, the muscles in her left leg pulsing from the tension. Robbie had the handbrake lever in his right hand and let it down. 'Gently lift your foot from the pedal and you should feel the biting point…'

She lifted her foot too quickly and the car shot forward, kangarooing to a halt. He pulled up the handbrake and looked a bit whiter than when they'd left home. 'Try again?' he winked at her.

'Do you think you'll find your real family?' Robbie wiped the grease from his mouth with the back of his hand. They'd made it to town for chips. Myrrh had been asked this question too many times, often by herself. She let him off the lecture about who she called *real*.

'Who knows?'

'If you do. I mean – if you decide to find them – I'll come with you if you like. I could drive you?' She imagined travelling around the world in his Capri, stopping off at campsites in search of her long-lost family. An adventure. She was sure he really meant it at the time. Even the goblin quietened down when she was around Robbie. She never forgot how sincere he was.

She watched him drive off in his precious car. Green like the grass verge. Green like a rotting finger. Green like a jealous goblin.

CAYENNE

He turns to me as we lay in bed. 'What are you doing with this old man?' An odd phrasing. Is he questioning me or disclosing his insecurities? Probably both. This episode has identified the controlling aspect of his nature. I feel an ache in my abdomen and the slick arrival of my period but ignore it and let the blood smear my thighs.

In the morning the sheets are stained red. My blood has soaked through to the mattress.

MYRRH

Myrrh always thought she was being watched as she grew up; it was part of her nature. She had read of hyperattentiveness, a trait of many adoptees, haunting them throughout their life. She had an uncanny ability to sense threats, often when they weren't even close by. But she could equally suspect everyone of doing her harm or plotting behind her back. When she was younger, she used to think people were looking at her because she was special or because she was a princess who had been kidnapped and sold at birth. Strangers would gawp right at her until she caught their eyes, then they'd look away. It wasn't even just passing glances; people openly stared at her.

As she grew older, paranoia flipped her princess fantasy on its head. She thought they were looking at dirt on her face or a tail growing from her behind or horns bursting from her scalp. She once asked Robbie if he noticed people looking at her when they were hanging out, but he just mumbled something about her being nice to look at, as if that was sufficient explanation. He was too shy or naïve then to really tell her what she needed to hear. People can't help but look at something that stands out; she had been marked out as different from the beginning of her life.

It had never dawned on her before; she never had to fill out questionnaires about ethnic origin to join the Guides or when she applied for a job scrubbing dishes at the local pub. She had a black doll: the only doll she found interesting, not because of its colour but because of its smooth, hard features and glossy eyelashes. But Myrrh was not black. She was mixed-race. And her family were not.

One morning on the way to school, she'd been sprayed liberally by a rook. She remembered the hard pelt and thud of it smacking her head and ricocheting off the loose hood hanging at the back of her neck.

'Myrrh's been shit on,' snorted Daryl, a grubby runt from the council houses, and he flicked his hands to make a cracking sound with his fingers while doing a little dance in disgust. 'Gross! It's slid down her neck.'

'Good luck, that is,' said Alice, as Myrrh made a quick dash into the shop.

Then Daryl said something that she'd never forget: 'If you were white, it would've blended in.' She dismissed the comment, laughed it off. She knew she wasn't black like Lenny Henry or the old man who lived next door to her grandparents in Bristol. So, if she wasn't black and she wasn't white, what colour was she supposed to be? And what did it all mean anyway when she was clueless as to what her biological parents actually looked like?

The only other adopted kid she was aware of was a boy in her school year called Michael, and he lived in the village too. His skin was paler than hers, but his hair curled up in tight rings against his head, and his eyes were the colour of the bay horses that used to graze in the field across from her bedroom window. He was a loner who used to lock himself in the toilet at break times with a book. On the bus he'd sit alone, shoulder pressed against the window. Sometimes, as if sleep were his favourite pastime, he would nod forward, bashing his forehead on the metal seat bar in front. She'd watch him, wondering if he had the same feeling of displacement. She wanted to ask him if he felt the same confusion bubbling up from inside and the frustration at not being able to explain it to everyone else. She wanted to ask him if a goblin taunted him.

She wanted to know if his goblin made him do things, like slice the tyres on Daryl's BMX with a penknife.

CAYENNE

She is his daughter [smack in the face]
He is her father [smack in the face]
They are related by blood [smack, smack]
And I am not [smack, smack, smack]

I am washing her silk blouses when I realise my hands have clenched it so tight that the fabric has started to loosen from the seams. With a quick tug I have ripped the seam so it is beyond repair. Her favourite blue blouse. I stuff it behind the wardrobe, still damp, hiding it away like I hide my growing hatred for her.

My hand touches the cool metal of a zip and I drag out the case. I open it to reveal neat, unworn baby clothes, knitted baby booties, and bottles.

MYRRH

Fragments of the dream remained in the morning when she woke. A rush of wings, blackened by soot, charred and ripped like an old tarpaulin. When Myrrh tried to breathe, she inhaled plumes of acrid smoke. And just as she was gasping for her last breath, a face, wrinkled and disfigured, leered at her. She could hardly make it out through the thick smog. The face grimaced, young and old at the same time, a hideous mash-up of sinew, bone and teeth. A baby's face yet aged.

Batting it away, she heard noises like fractured words spill from its slick mouth. A river of putrid milk gushed from the creature's neck. Its bony fingers threatened to embrace her. It spat caul-smeared kisses.

'Feed me,' it screeched.

SANDRA

Part of her wanted him to say he'd had an awful time, the people were rude, the location dreadful, but he was beaming in that infuriating way people do when they've had an adventure. She smiled as he bounded towards her from the arrivals gate, the screen sliding open like a seventies game show to reveal not a celebrity but her husband of thirty years. He gathered her up in a showy embrace and she nearly choked as his arm pressed across her neck. There was a smell – aftershave? perfume? – pungent and dampening on his collar.

'Did you miss me?' He was first to ask even though she thought it more apt for her to ask him the same question. Did he ever miss her on those long weekends filled with – what were they filled with?

'You know I do. I always do.' She instinctively started wheeling his case across the crowded arrivals hall, his other bag hooked over her shoulder.

'Traffic not too bad? Did Sally help with the directions?'

She bristled slightly at the mention of a woman's name. Sally. He'd named the satnav after taking it on several journeys alone.

'I didn't use it on the way up, to be honest,' she lied.

'Why not, love? That's what she's there for. She's got me out of a few pickles when I've met a diversion or two.' How did he do that? How did he make her feel so utterly helpless in an instant?

They reached the car, and he loaded his case and bag into the boot before settling in to the passenger seat. He plugged the satnav back in to the cigarette lighter and switched it on. It took an age for the display to light up.

'I can drive if you want.' He looked over but was already buckling his seatbelt across his middle and undoing the top of his flies. 'Ah, it's good to be back on home soil,' he sighed and pushed the lever to recline his seat back. Home soil: what was that? Where was that? He had made this place his home, built a family with her, but she still couldn't reconcile the shock all those years ago. Did he lead another life? Was she a fool?

'*At the next roundabout, take the second exit…*'

'I'm not going to do that,' Sandra said. 'We'll be driving round and round the airport.'

'*Take the second exit…*'

'She'll recalculate once you're on the main road,' he said.

'Just as well I know which direction to head then, isn't it?' The maze of lanes to exit the airport made her head throb, and he was chattering about someone he met who turned out to be marvellous company but who at first impressions he thought he was a twit. It was the middle of the mountains. 'Idyllic,' he said. 'The sort of place you could fall in love.' Did he say fall in love or fall in love with? She indicated right and switched lanes.

'*Keep left…*'

'Damn.' She checked her mirrors and indicated left and switched lanes again.

'You need to get in the right lane, love.' He held his hand up as if that would help guide the car.

'I know, I know – turn that bloody thing off.' She indicated again and swerved, narrowly avoiding a car overtaking her.

The motorway was closed when she made her way up to collect him, and she ended up on a massive diversion down country lanes, and that annoying voice kept telling her to '*TURN AROUND*

WHEN POSSIBLE.' It was too late. She had the opportunity to turn around and head to a different destination. Her life could have so easily turned a different corner when she opened *that* letter at the very start of their relationship. *You have been named as the father...*

'They didn't have those flashing signs when I came up.'

'Keep going. I'm sure Sally knows the best route.' He reached to switch the satnav back on and she gritted her teeth.

She had not slept well. She never did when he was away from home. Not having enough sleep makes the world seem sharp and dangerous. No one else cares about your lack of sleep, about your own body clock. They are looking out of their own eyes, following their own diversions, too busy to notice your eyes open like cartoon-cat eyes, saucers on stalks.

They were going home. The home they had nurtured together, raised their two sons in, spilt wine over soft furnishings in and layered with skin cells, infused with the unique scent of their family. She shared it over half her life with him. He may have forgotten the acid burn of betrayal resting like a veil over their heads just before their wedding

You have been named as the father

but she had not forgotten a thing.

For now though, she was driving them home.

CAYENNE

Blood is thicker than water. She said that to my face. What she didn't realise is that the correct saying is: *The blood of the covenant is thicker than the water of the womb*. Rarely have I heard anyone use it correctly. The bonds we make by choice are much more important than blood ties, like family. Why does it always get twisted in favour of the family? Family has only ever brought me grief. But when I have my own child, then I might use the same phrase on her, smiling into her simple, little face. Yes, blood might just be thicker than water. We'll see.

SANDRA

Sandra looked at the photograph again. Why had this stranger contacted her son claiming they were related? Why had she not contacted her husband directly? Although she was certain that had the girl – no, she wasn't a girl anymore – contacted her husband directly he would have ignored her letter. She had lived with him too long to know that a strain of obstinacy coursed through his veins. He was too expressly focused on what he wanted to pay any attention to someone else's motivations.

The girl's eyes are remarkably similar, thought Sandra. Or was she seeking similarities that were not there? Resemblances exist between a whole host of unrelated people; it didn't mean they shared genes. But the unmistakable shape of this young woman's nose, her skin, even the way her head faced front on as she looked into the camera, reminded Sandra of her husband.

She had been researching her own genealogy, as an amateur, and discovered that her late grandfather had died not knowing his father. This saddened her. She remembered thinking how awful he must've felt growing up without a face to identify with. She felt some wrongdoing had occurred even if she were not directly involved.

Every child deserves to know where they come from; every person deserves to know who they are related to. These basic tenets were something she had felt very strongly about for years. Yet, when faced with the possibility that her husband was not owning up to his actions, the viewpoint shifted out of focus. The fact that it was years ago, and the child had now grown into a woman, didn't soften the sinking feeling in her gut. If the dates added up, the child would've been conceived during that first passionate year her husband had courted her. He'd been so full of fire and promise back then, as if she would set alight as he whisked her from party to party introducing her to colleagues, the two of them planning their bright future together.

She regretted burning all her old diaries. Now her mind scoured back through time to remember when they were apart: what opportunities he may have had to visit the mother of this child, stilted conversations on the phone, the letter that appeared like a portent weeks before their wedding day stating that he had been named as the father, the accusations, the dread, the eventual settling for trust and truth. That trust once again put to the test.

Do most people prefer someone else to tell them what to do? There may be answers, but was a resolution ever possible when an unknown relative resurfaced like old dogma? Moving away seemed like a mutual decision at the time but was probably his idea, if Sandra were honest. The trajectory of his career took precedence in their new, young household. But she was the one with the family to leave behind, having grown up in the area with parents who were half expecting grandchildren on their doorstep. He had already left his family behind in Egypt when he emigrated to England to continue his studies. She admired his tenacity. They met at work after all. That was how she first saw him: a professional man with a quiet strength.

Perhaps it was fate that meant she opened his post while he was working away. That letter could have broken them apart, there and then, stopped their plans stone-cold dead. It was a big deal. Getting married, making a life with someone, then committing to follow that person wherever their career took them. She knew about duty. But this felt like humiliation at the starting line, like she had been tripped up before the pistol was fired.

It was odd reading his name on that letter all those years ago.

You have been named as the father of her baby.

She re-read it, almost aghast at the implications of it, but a seed of doubt lodged itself in her brain. How could she ignore such a blatant allegation? Her initial instinct was to catch the train and confront him, to demand an explanation from him, face to face. She knew if she phoned him, the sharp edge to her voice would give her away, he would wrangle out of her what was bothering her, and she would not have an opportunity to study his expression.

Social Services did not have time to play pranks. The letter seemed official enough on headed paper with the name and contact details of the assigned social worker. She read each word on the succinct typed letter, again and again, until it consumed her all morning and she knew it by heart.

You have been named.

Father of her baby.

Moments after she first read the letter she found there were no trains leaving in the next few hours, so when she exhausted all options of waiting to speak with him in person she rang his work number.

'What do you mean *news*?' He sounded tired. His long working hours dripped down the telephone line.

She was trying to hold back the tears, fighting the urge to scream at him, accuse him of sleeping with other women, of lying to her, tricking her into a marriage. In hindsight, that might have been the best course of action.

'Sandra, I'm busy right now – what is it? Is it your mother?'

She choked with anger when he mentioned her mother. Why did it always have to be *her* problem? She ended up blurting everything out. She read him the letter in hushed tones, her jaw

MYRRH

tense, afraid the walls might hear. She almost choked as she read the words, 'named as the father', when they had not even begun to plan *their* family together.

'I don't know what to say. Listen, I'll take some leave, come home early. We can talk.' He sounded less tired now, more desperate. She wasn't sure what there was to talk about. It was either true or not true. If it was true then it would blow all her plans – their plans – sky high. She could not even confide in a friend. The wedding was weeks away. She had planned to wear her own mother's wedding dress. His family couldn't attend, but they were going to visit his relatives in Egypt afterwards to receive their blessing. All these arrangements, the flowers, the church, the venue, the food, the invitations with their embossed initials were all flooding in and out of focus. It had to be a mistake. Who was this woman anyhow? He had never mentioned a serious relationship before. He had never mentioned anyone.

CAYENNE

A few days without the tense atmosphere of his daughter's car-crash loaded presence. It has been bliss. She flies in and flies out, blatantly ignoring me and not even saying 'hello'. She did not even give me eye contact and I was not in the mood for small talk. I feel an impending doom, a nervousness that churns up my guts as if I am returning to an old wound or battleground. It is not a pleasant feeling, and even though I know there is little reason to be troubled by her, I still feel like an outsider or intruder in my own home.

Once, a squirrel got inside the house through an open window. It went crazy. Have you ever seen a contained creature that cannot find its way out? It is like watching a series of badly choreographed dances, perfect stillness combined with an unleashing of kinetic fury of fur, claws and teeth. Random chattering flight like the particles of the universe condensed down into one small being. Scratches everywhere. It darted behind the cushions, then decimated the umbrella I used to try and control its erratic movement. It dived inside my shoes and dragged dust from beneath the refrigerator with its bushy tail.

The look on her face winds me up as does the motion of her arrogant little head and that insolent stare that she saves just for me. Does he not know she is going with boys? I can see the shadows under her eyes, the way she pulls her collar up to hide the nibble marks on her neck, the way she rolls her hips when she walks.

I killed the squirrel. Then dumped its body in the woods.

SANDRA

It is early evening and the kitchen diner still smells of roasted meat and garlic. They are sitting around the table, a family conference. Middle class. Civilised and tense. The sort of family to hold meetings or gatherings even when the children were too young to sit and appreciate the delicacies of discussion or debate. There are snacks in bowls, olives or salted pretzels, and a jug of cordial with glasses on the table so people can help themselves. A small joke is muttered as they all take their places, each having a preferred setting for mealtimes, a passing around of the jug, a few coughs.

'Shall we start?' the woman says, kicking off proceedings. 'It's best if we air it all in the open.' She wears a tailored trouser suit and flats. She casually moves around the room in clean lines. Her hair is always styled; she books a regular four-weekly appointment with Bridie at Bridie's Salon. That, and her nails, currently a shade called *Moonlight Romance*, which does not reflect her current mood.

The husband shuffles his hands, lines up the dishes in the centre of the table but does not eat any of the snacks.

'Have you had any more emails from her?' the eldest son is asked. He is in his thirties, with tired eyes, slightly paunchy, pale skin capable of tanning if he spent less time in the office.

'No, just a reply last month.'

The other son, younger by only a few years, sits and places his hands on the edge of the table. 'You can find almost anyone on the internet,' he says. 'It's virtually impossible to remove any of the data. Once it's on there, it's there to stay.' He takes a handful of nuts in his palm and tips the lot into his mouth.

'Sam, do you want to say anything?' Sandra looks at her husband fiddling with the tablecloth and bites back her impatience.

He sighs. They all wait. The younger son takes a pretzel and crunches it loudly, then another, until Sam looks up and past him to the cabinet of glasses on the wall. The son slows his chewing and tries to muffle the sound amid the silent pause.

'It was obviously a long time ago. The dates don't add up. I had left the hospital by then.'

'The one in Chester?' the older boy asks.

'Cornwall. I worked there when I first came over to the UK.' He continues, still unable to meet his son's eyes, 'She was a bit obsessed with me.'

'Obsessed how?' the elder boy asks.

'Stalker.' The younger laughs then shoves more nuts in his mouth.

'No, not a stalker. But she was a bit needy. Wanted to meet all the time. She was working at the hospital. I think she was lonely.'

'Did you go out with her… I mean, have a relationship?' The elder boy looks at his mother's ashen face. She is using her elbows to prop herself up on the table. How many times has she has rehearsed her lines? How many times has she heard the script of his father's life, his urgent pleading before they got married, which turned into the cocksure reticence of a man who is confident he will not be found out? She is listening to every single word he says, scouring each syllable for a clue, for the truth.

'She was a nurse at the hospital…'

'You already said that,' the younger son chips in.

'Let me finish.' The impatience in Sam's voice seeping through. 'There were lots of nurses at the hospital, there were lots of doctors. I think she has mistaken me for someone else.'

'She named you as the father of her child,' the wife says as if the words might curse her. 'Why would she do that if it weren't true?' Her body is rigid and she begins to feel the nagging pulse of a tension headache at her temples.

'Have we got a sister? I'd really like a sister.' The younger son grins.

The elder looks at his younger brother, sighs.

'You don't have a sister.' Sam hisses the word 'sister' as if it were a venomous snake that might strike. He cannot bring himself to say the word 'daughter', to even associate such a relationship with this awkward situation.

'Why would she say it's you? I just don't get it.' The older boy addresses his dad but looks over at his brother. 'Wasn't it all a bit – you know – free and easy back in the seventies?'

'I remember very little from that time. We're talking over thirty years ago. A lot has happened since then.'

'No,' Sam says. 'It doesn't add up. There's not a chance she could be…' He slams his hand down on the table, making the glasses rattle. Sandra draws in a sharp breath.

'We just thought it best to discuss this, well, in case she got it in her head to turn up here.'

'But she's not contacted you?' the older boy asks.

'No.'

'What are the chances of her turning up here then?'

'People think it's their right to search out long-lost family. They think they can just waltz in and become a part of something when they have no right.'

'Well why shouldn't they, why shouldn't she? You're the one who always bangs on about women's rights.' The elder boy stands up and leaves the room.

The younger son follows his brother's movements then snaps back to face the parents.

The elder boy comes back into the room, 'I don't know why we're even talking about it if Dad says it's not true.' There is a hint of disappointment in his voice.

The younger boy stands, grabbing a handful of snacks from the table, and exits the room, leaving his parents silently staring at the table.

Sandra breaks the silence. 'I know we've been through this before, but you do realise I need to ask you these questions.'

'I know,' he says. An old wound has been torn open. The lifeblood of their relationship is gushing out everywhere.

'Are you sure? One hundred percent sure she is not your daughter?'

Slick, red blood laps at their ankles. Unstoppable, possibly fatal.

'We've been through the dates; she can't be.'

Blood rises rapidly up their calves to their knees.

'This woman named you as the father of her child. She must have thought it was you.'

The warmth and stickiness envelops them as they sit rigid on their chairs.

'It's just a name on a piece of paper.'

Their lungs fill with a viscous mess.

'It's your name.'

They are gasping for breath.

'It changes nothing.'

They are drowning.

These are the moments that define us. The irrepressible, the inconceivable, the inconsiderable weight. The unexpected, the cut of life. Guts spilled out. The crush. The punch.

The elder son listens in to his parents' conversation. He has held his own in some tricky meetings at work but nothing has prepared him for this. He can hear his mother and father still having their discussion in heightened, guttural tones in the kitchen. Was she weeping? This was a big deal. They'd had their arguments before, and there were times in his childhood when he could feel the silences permeate the walls. But this was on another scale of family disruption. He knew that much.

Like a magic trick he suddenly may have a sister he has never met. A secret that has been kept or… not even kept, more like ignored. Even though his father denies any involvement, instinctively he knows his father lied. Like the time he came home early from college to find a woman leaving the house. Not a friend of his mother's or a work colleague, but a younger, attractive woman who paused to slowly kiss his father on the lips before jauntily skipping back to her car and waving him goodbye as he shut the front door. When he did eventually gain the nerve to put his key in the lock, his father was returning downstairs with his slippers on, carrying a bundle of washing, whistling cheerfully.

There was no confrontation. Just a sorry look that passed between them and the familiar gush of water arriving to wash away all evidence.

CAYENNE

There are times in life when passion rests ripe and abundant, when grain swells and tips the heads of corn in reverential bows, trees balloon in full-bodied coats of emerald, the sky warms the earth, and the waters quench the edges of the riverbank, tickling the fish with fine underwater currents. There are moods best suited to the ripening end of summer when flowing robes and fruity apparel swarm around soft sun-kissed bodies. But the dark summer sky at dusk reminds me of pomegranates. I used to pluck their seeds from their webbed nest with a cocktail stick and crunch them between my teeth.

I want a man so full of fertile seed that even sitting next to him will open me up like a blossoming flower so he can pollinate me. So, on a cool autumnal day, I pack my bag and go to meet another man. This man might give me what I want.

MYRRH

'It's not fair.' Myrrh slammed the door with such intensity that a splinter of wood dislodged from the frame and landed on the linoleum. 'Why did you have to arrange it when it's Robbie's birthday?'

Her mum's face collapsed as the words were spat at her. Robbie would be fourteen before Myrrh, his birthday falling in March. She wanted to spend it with him. Only it was the Easter holidays, and she always stayed with her grandparents over Easter.

'You like going to Nan and Grandad's.' Her mum wiped the dishes and stacked them on the kitchen worktop. All the dishes were different, some with flowers and others with bold geometric patterns. Nothing matched, not even the cutlery. She placed a dish carefully inside another and turned to look at her daughter. 'Why don't you go and see Robbie before you leave?'

She knew her mum wasn't offering her full attention because *The Archers* was on the radio. She had this sort of look when she half-listened to the radio play, like her eyes were watching the actors in her head, following their movements as they spoke the story.

Myrrh picked up the splinter of wood, which was shaped like a cocktail stick, from the floor and put it in her pocket and hoped her dad wouldn't notice the damage when he got home. He'd go mental. She had some craft glue somewhere and could probably fix it without him knowing. Ironically, if she hadn't damaged the door frame she would never have found her adoption paperwork. The sudden rush of anger followed by apathy had left her chilly.

She went to fetch her mum's fleecy jumper, the one that made her look like a sheep, because it was really warm, and all her jumpers were either in the wash basket or not yet dry. As she rummaged around in the wardrobe she discovered an unusual-looking tin full of old typed documents, like a shrine encased in fluffy woollens. Her memory could play tricks on her sometimes. Just like her goblin did.

lies, all lies

She seemed to remember emotions – especially the nasty ones – more than experiences, yet she could hardly remember the names of people she went to school with when she was fourteen. But she couldn't forget Liza Edwards. Her bullying was not discerning in that she picked on everyone in some way or another. Myrrh was probably an easy target.

'Oi! Katrina. That's your real name ain't it?' She had jet black hair and a mole on her top lip. ('A beauty mark' she called it, but it was just a mole.) No one ever called her Katrina except teachers on the first day, until she told them she was called Myrrh.

'What d'you say Kat? Katty. Can I call you Katty?' She thrust her face close, her breath minty and sour from chewing gum.

Myrrh remained silent. Anger bubbled inside her. The mean cow. Why was she letting her speak to her that way?

smack her down
she deserves a whack
break her arm
watch it splinter

'What's it feel like being adopted? You're adopted, ain't you?' Her lip curled up in a sneer, and her tone implied it was an impediment, something to be ashamed of.

you're adopted ain't you?

you're unwanted ain't you?

flawed

damaged

bad

smack her stupid button nose

'I don't know what it's like to *not* be adopted.' A sudden surge of bravado made her face up to Liza. It was one subject she was confident speaking about. It was on occasions like these that she was glad the goblin was ready for a fight.

fight, fight, fight, fight

'But I mean, your *real* mum and dad didn't want you, did they?' Liza was pushing the boundaries, beginning to sound a lot like Goblin.

Myrrh hated it when people referred to her birth parents as *real* rather than her adoptive parents. Her real mum and dad were the ones who had brought her up. Not the strangers Liza was referring to. It stung her but she said nothing, squeezing her hands into fists, pressing her nails into her palms. There was nothing real about them. She didn't even know what they looked like.

'Was it because you smell?' Liza held her nose between her forefinger and thumb.

she deserves a smacking now

stupid, fucking bitch

'Or because you're a loser?'

rip her eyes out

grab her throat with your nails

make her bleed

Liza turned to walk away, nose pointed in the air. She was flanked by two sycophants who trailed behind her like a loose piece of cotton. How could someone like that even have friends who stuck around?

do it

do it

do it

Myrrh felt the rage engulf her whole body. With an action a bully would be proud of, Myrrh rushed at Liza and shoved her full on with both hands to the centre of her back. Liza went sprawling flat on her face. She didn't even have time to put her hands out, and her head took the full brunt. Smack. Myrrh heard Liza's face hit the tarmac of the school playground.

When she reflected on this moment some years later, she caught a sliver of the feeling that ran through her that day. It was not shame at causing someone harm, but great exhilaration. She may have even laughed in those first few moments after it happened. Until she saw the blood, and the shocked looks on her classmate's faces who had appeared to witness the assault. This wasn't her fault. She didn't like hurting people. She was a good person. But what if she wasn't? What if she had inherited more than hair colour, or eye colour, and the shape of her nose? What if she had inherited something much, much worse?

nice one, nice one

The goblin leapt about so hard that all she could do was run and run and get far away from everything.

everyone gets what they deserve

in the happily ever after

CAYENNE

I arrived early at their house and waited in the shabby kitchen while he went upstairs to change his clothes. We had agreed to meet by an ancient hill fort, chosen because of its relatively secluded location, but his wife was feeling under the weather, so I met them in their home. This was more private anyhow.

While I waited, I leaned on the kitchen worktop surveying the crumbs and discarded crockery from breakfast. Knives and spoons piled on plates and mugs with the dregs of cold tea in the sink.

I fidgeted around the room trying not to pry, taking in piles of letters, a large wooden table smeared with food stains, a window that looked out to the sloping lawn and an apple tree ripe with fruit. The tap was dripping and I resisted the urge to reach for it and make it stop.

Then, my eyes rested on two jars of fig jam standing sentinel, as if her womb and his heart had been boiled up together, left to cool and set behind glass. Those two jars, waiting silently to be opened and spread out, ingested and transformed, rang out with an omen. Before I could stop myself, I picked one up and opened the lid with a satisfying pop then felt self-conscious at having opened something that did not belong to me.

Expecting to see a sticky freshness, I was surprised to see

that beneath their sealed lids a festering mould was beginning to bloom. I heard the stairs creak, so quickly resealed the lid and replaced the jar where I had found it.

Both of them stood side by side smiling nervously at me. We knew the first meeting would be awkward, even in their own home. But it was a necessary formality. The house was so silent, and the ticking of the grandfather clock in the hallway was starting to irritate me.

'So –' I thought it best to kick things off '– have you lived here long?'

They looked at one another as if I had asked them something that needed translating.

'Miss, we'd prefer to just get this over with and discuss the possibilities of you having our child for us.'

'Sure, sure.' I nodded and picked up a pink wafer, dunking it in my tea then regretting my actions as they stared at me. I wasn't even sure if surrogacy was legal, but I'm sure they had researched all sorts of options before finding me.

The agreement was we would meet and see if there was chemistry, and, if so, he would provide the 'donation'. His wife had agreed that it should be at their home so the initial act was in a familiar place should the action be successful. We didn't talk about money. That would come later. I didn't tell him there was no way they'd keep the baby.

'Do you know your cycle?' she asked.

'My cycle?'

'Are you regular? We need to know this won't take too long. We've waited a long time.' She bowed her head to her lap. Why did these women act like wet rags? Waiting didn't produce babies; I knew that well enough.

'Listen,' I said as I took another pink wafer, 'I'm on the same page. Trust me. I'll need some money up front though. For good food…'

'We have cash.'

I smiled and looked around their sitting room with its heavy brocade curtains and dark, heavy antique furniture. This was turning out to be too easy.

They offered me soup, but I couldn't bear another minute in their miserable company. I became increasingly aware of his hands and arms, as if they were a separate entity that might suddenly lift him into flight. I kept trying to imagine them actually fucking, or him depositing his lukewarm cache into a jug and her handing a turkey baster directly to me.

It took all of my willpower not to retch.

We discussed all the ways for maximum efficiency and higher probability of the sperm reaching their target. No matter what came before or after this moment, I felt as if I was destined to be a mother with limitless power, like an endless battalion of white horses crashing against the sea defences. One wave expiring as another seven took its place, with some becoming beasts of white stature – stallions, war horses, strong fighters – and some melting in the spume, milk-white foals swallowed in the grey soup of the ocean.

I was caught in a momentary daydream of my ghost lover, him reaching some deep place within me, a gentle teasing of each other's edges. If a soul was going to incarnate in my body then I would claim it as my own, not give it away to strangers. All I could imagine were the eyes of my ghost lover; every thought, every action, every future plan, every song, every breath, leans towards him.

'Miss?' They were looking at me intently. I must've drifted off. It was stifling hot in their house. I tugged at my neckerchief to loosen it and rubbed at the sweat on my upper lip. They exchanged an unreadable glance and both stood at the same time.

'We'll be in touch.' He guided me by the elbow towards the front door.

I think they felt sorry for me. *They*, the desperate losers, felt sorry for *me*. I wanted to smash their festering rotten homemade jars of jam over their ridiculous heads. I wanted to hurt him because he gave his wife loving glances and touched her gently on her arm. He had a wife and what did I have? A reluctant used-up old man and his spoilt daughter who made it clear I was unwelcome in their life.

MYRRH

'Is it true?' Robbie grinned at her, flashing his braces like a Bond villain. He was playing on his Commodore 64, sending the racing car over smooth tracks, mimicking the car noises as it accelerated or turned a corner.

'Robbie. I don't want to talk about it.'

'But it was you, wasn't it?'

'Who told you?'

'Everyone knows. They said you broke her nose. It's bloody mint.' He hammered away at the keys with his fingers.

'I just came round to tell you I won't be here on your birthday.'

Robbie stopped playing and looked up at her, the tinny sound of metal crashing as he let the game end prematurely.

'Mum's arranged for me to go to Nan and Grandad's. I'd rather be with you, but I can't really get out of it.'

'It's no big deal anyway,' he said, pushing his glasses back up his nose with the heel of his hand, a gesture that said the opposite.

'No, right.' Myrrh shuffled awkwardly. 'So, I'll see you when I get back then?'

There was a police car on her driveway when she walked back from Robbie's house. She had to squeeze by to get in the back gate because the car had been parked so tight to the fence.

As she opened the porch door, she heard voices in the kitchen. One was her mum's.

'…cross that bridge when we come to it. What can we do about it?'

Shit. Shit. Shit. They're talking about me, thought Myrrh.

She froze and waited in the porch, in limbo between the kitchen door and the porch door, still ajar, but monumentally squeaky even with the slightest movement. They must have heard her open it.

'…unlikely to be a problem…' another woman said, her voice high pitched and posh.

'…there shouldn't be any connection…'

'…has she mentioned anything?'

Oh God. She'd be forced to confess. There was no way she could lie to her mum.

The woman was offered another cup of tea. Myrrh heard the rattle of teacups.

'No, I'd best be going.' Their voices grew louder and a chair squeaked on the kitchen floor.

'Please let me know,' her mum said, her voice loaded with angst. Myrrh was poised, ready to look like she'd just arrived if they opened the back door. But her Mum took the visitor to the front door, which she thought oddly formal.

CAYENNE

When I return home I clean upstairs, strip off my clothes, free and relaxed, knowing we are alone. I walk downstairs naked, breaking the coolness that has been evident between us for several days. He regards me with that impenetrable look of his, but I see something shift in his features, like a slit of light breaking through a dark sky. I have a long shower and clean the bathroom and light some incense.

When I return downstairs, this time in my gown, I find he has placed cheese and crackers on the table, and we pour some wine and sit on the couch together. It is a rare gift to sit together alone in the house without the pressure of her. Even when she is there, just flashing in and out, I feel anxious. She starts moving things around in the kitchen, trying to make her presence known by rearranging the angle of the tea pot, moving pans from one side of the stove to the other.

We go to bed and make love. His heavy groin pounds into me and sweat pools at the base of his spine as he grinds his seed into me. I let my fingers slide over the slick of his back and daydream about my ghost lover. After he has rolled off me, I slide my pillow under my buttocks to tilt my pelvis and keep any liquid inside me. I must have drifted off to sleep because when I wake the morning chorus of birds is like a klaxon outside our window.

MYRRH

The sun shines hot and sharp, so after breakfast I bake some flapjacks, clean out the fridge, vacuum downstairs and wash the dishes while he tends to his paperwork. Calm, tranquillity, and harmony descends on the place once more. We are back on track and sit outside together for lunch. I don't even think about babies or the future.

MYRRH

Ginger was picking something orange and crusty off her cardigan sleeve, inspecting it with a scrutiny usually reserved for crime scenes rather than suspect stains.

'I think it's baked bean, or it could be butternut squash.' She sniffed her finger cautiously. Myrrh imagined her at home, feeding her brood, clearing up, standing in her kitchen, a busy hub of chaos with toys littering the hallway, noise and laughter, squabbles and *'Put that away!'*, *'What have I told you!'*, *'Dinner's ready! Come and get it!'*. All the restless normality of a young family, working parents. Millions of juggled demands.

'Do you ever wonder what your purpose is?' Myrrh asked her.

She laughed. 'Bloody dogsbody: that's what my purpose is.'

'I'm serious, Ginny.'

'Never really thought about it. To live my life and be happy I suppose.'

'What if you're living the wrong life? Like, what if there was some kind of accident?'

'What's wrong, Myrrh?' She looked up, concern wrinkling her forehead.

'I get these feelings. Like something doesn't quite fit.'

lies, all lies

'What do you mean?' Ginger screwed up her face.

'It's hard to explain. I feel a bit... possessed.'
name me
'Christ!'
'Not like that. Well, sort of –'
get a life
get your own life
'What do you mean? You've got a lovely home, family who love you, a job working with the most attractive person –' She flicked her hair back, stuck out her chest, and pouted. Myrrh felt her lip quiver, tears sting her eyes. Nothing seemed to satisfy her; she was always searching for something to fill that missing part, always trying to feed the goblin.

'Myrrh, listen. Everyone thinks the grass is greener, but what if it's just grass?'

'It's just sometimes I feel like I should be somewhere else, be someone else. I think I'm missing the point of my own life.' Always in the slipstream, she never really felt she was part of anything, even her own family, *especially* her own family.

not your family

Ginger stood up and faced her, taking Myrrh's hands in her own. It felt odd holding hands with her friend now they were adults. 'What do you want, Myrrh?' she asked with a sincerity that made Myrrh feel uncomfortable.

'I want to live by the sea, paint, fall in love...'

'You do live by the sea, and you're really good at painting... look, you never see the tricky bits of other people's lives, all the messy crap they hide behind a smile... Nobody's perfect. We're just people doing the best we can.'

Myrrh let her friend's hands slip from her grasp.

'I'm fine. It's nothing really.' Myrrh let out a sigh but felt churning inside. She tried a smile but even to herself it felt empty. If she couldn't tell her best friend what was going on, she may as well not tell anyone. She felt like a passenger in her own life.

Myrrh looked at Ginger's face. Ginger seemed to know who she was, what her life was about. It highlighted how the ground beneath her own feet always felt shaky as if she were walking on shifting sands. She thought of holidays by the sea, standing on the shoreline, waves lapping over her ankles, sandy water washing over the tops of her feet, and the sensation that it was her moving and not the water. How transient it all was. The sand and the waves and the planet moved. No matter how reliable or secure it all seemed, nothing ever remained the same.

CAYENNE

My ghost lover does not need to know the finer details of my life, its ups and downs. We do not converse.

The wife wishes to meet me again to discuss whether I am to have their baby. It is a Wednesday and there are things she'd like to know. I want to observe how she moves, find out the inner workings of their marriage. A dangerous game, but I am drawn to it, although the bitter taste in my mouth won't go away.

'There is only the business at hand,' I tell the wife.

The wife casts her eyes downward.

'I know this sounds strange, and I know you've come all this way, but could we have another think about it and get back to you?' Her pursed lips imply I am one in a long line of girls they have interviewed for the position.

'We really like how you look,' she says, brandishing her wedding ring, testing it with her thumb as if it were an itch.

'Thanks,' I reply through gritted teeth. 'I guess it's easier if the baby looks like you both.' I had read this on a leaflet.

The wife sniffs and takes a gulp of her coffee. There is a taste of metal in the air between us, a taste we both swallow awkwardly.

'It's really important that our baby is related to us – well, at least one of us.' The wife laughs nervously.

I sense her desperation. It's uncomfortable to watch. I do not feel the sentiment of the statement below her breasts, in her gut, in her groin. Part of me wants to spit back my own image of her husband, grunting over a kitchen jug ready to impregnate me.

I make a note to get more money up front from these desperate idiots.

I sip the too-sweet coffee and let the uncomfortable silence fill up the room like noxious gas. What more can I say?

'It's ironic,' the wife says, 'but since we've been meeting you, I find he meets some part of me he's been unable to before.'

I stand up and tip the remains of my coffee in her lap, hoping it is still hot enough to scald her cunt.

'We really are glad you've come.' She smiles up at me.

I punch her dopey husband in the face until blood splashes from his nose onto their carpet.

He smiles back at me too.

As I leave the room, the contents of my mug sit untouched on the table. The couple sit very, very still. I let the corners of my mouth move just enough to hint at a confident smile and assuage their doubts about me.

MYRRH

Myrrh held on to the belief that she was wanted and, by some distressing social mores, her birth mother felt goaded into giving her baby away. Sometimes she daydreamed that her birth mother had been horrifically murdered. There was hidden strength in that belief. What it meant was, if you don't know how someone feels about you, it's up to you to convince yourself they cared.

Amid the crashing turmoil of uncertainty, she had lucid moments of feeling secure, knowing she was loved by parents who'd adopted her as their own. But they only knew her adopted persona; it was like buying a living, working model of something natural, like a tree, but knowing that it was not the real thing, that it was only something by design.

She devoured stories as if they might hold the key to the missing part of her own story. Characters and settings were integrated into her own made-up persona: one week she would be Rapunzel trapped in a tower by a wicked witch, the next she would reimagine herself as the daughter of a proud man who sent her off to marry the king; in some she was the evil troll who spun straw into gold and demanded the firstborn child of a princess.

CAYENNE

She's washing up. The anger rises like bile up my throat. How can you carry out a task designed to clean items, yet make more of a mess by doing it? She doesn't think to stack all the dirty plates, cups and greasy pans on the side of the sink; instead she haphazardly grasps the nearest piece of crockery, dunking it in the water.

I see from the side of her face that she is grinning. She knows it is winding me up, knows how to infuriate me. It does. She thinks she has won this battle because the facts are: 1) She is doing the washing up *ergo* she is being helpful *ergo* she cannot be branded as a lazy layabout *ergo* she is a saint. 2) She is doing it because her father is in the kitchen reading his newspaper *ergo* she is performing just for him *ergo* she is daddy's little princess.

I pick up the heavy unwashed skillet, soiled with tomato juices, and calmly walk towards her. She still has her back to me and doesn't turn. She is swilling the water as she softly hums a nameless tune. The oily scent coming from the pan makes me retch. I grip the skillet handle with both hands. I slowly lift it high. My knuckles are bone white. She still does not notice me. I take aim. With one swift motion I smack it down onto her shining golden hair marvelling at the cracking sound of metal on bone. The sound echoes across the kitchen. The quick bloom of red on gold reminds me of sunsets. I watch the slow-motion crumple of her body to the floor. Feel the thud of my heartbeat. Then I hear a scrape as his chair pushes back across the flagstone tiles. His hands press hard on my hands, prying the weapon from my fingers.

He is saying my name over and over. 'Cayenne,' he says. 'Cayenne, what happened?' As I blink out of my trance, I see her still standing at the sink. She turns towards his voice, which has a tone edged with worry. My arms are rigid by my side, tomato juice dripping onto the linoleum. I taste the tang of blood as I realise I have bitten my tongue. I swallow the blood down as he takes the skillet from me and places it on the worktop.

'Princess, come and sit down.' He guides me to the nearest chair, gripping both of my arms from behind. As I glance back at her he doesn't see her smirk, but I do. She wipes her hands on a towel then casually tosses it on the table like she is throwing a match at a pool of petroleum.

MYRRH

There was an ongoing joke in her family that it always rained on her birthday, although it was the middle of summer. August seemed to chuck out fiendish weather in defiance of the summer holidays. Hordes of holidaymakers in cars and caravans backed up on the motorway spewing out fumes, a stream of traffic edging its way into the small coastal town containing families and couples looking to get away from it all. The green sweep of surrounding countryside seemed empty compared to the bustling arcades and greasy seaside chip shops.

With every birthday she was reminded how she still didn't have answers about her past. Had her birth mother moved? After the fruitless trip to Cornwall, and hours of searching online to find nothing, she could only assume that was the case. In the end, she'd written a letter to the same address, another lengthy composition, and endured days of pushing Goblin further and further back. The address on the birth certificate was so old, and so many years had gone by, that anything was possible, but she had supplied a return address in case the woman no longer lived there, and she'd seen from the tracking that the letter had been signed for. Though by whom, she didn't know.

Perhaps she had died.

your mother is a stiff little corpse

your mother smells of rot
your mother is not your mother

She tried to skip over the hideous thoughts but left them in the recesses of her brain as a possibility. Maybe she was dead, and her search was fruitless. She already had a stockpile of unknowns to wade through first without adding more substance to the ever-growing mound of loss.

When she tried to speak to her parents about it they closed up, couldn't say anything. *Aren't we enough?* Myrrh thought they said in their silence. *Aren't we all you need?* But there was something they were hiding. She could feel it. Not just the identity of the people who gave birth to her, but something else.

It made sense that her adoptive parents would protect her from the truth when she was a child, but she was old enough to cope with it now. What if she was the living proof that something good could come from something horrific? Who were these people named on her paperwork, and why was her birth father so adamant she wasn't his daughter?

CAYENNE

They have reneged on the deal. They say trust is paramount if we are to proceed. Something about things not adding up. Something about the stability of my home life. In short, they will not be going through with the surrogacy. Words like risk, expense, uncertainty, time, honesty. Pah! I don't really know why I even considered this was an option. I need to look after myself, not complicate matters with third parties. There is so much in my head right now.

I smash a tin of beans onto his sleeping skull.

His arms reflex automatically up above his head, and those dopey, puffy bagged eyes blink open like he's trying to strobe his way into seeing this live-action motion picture starring him.

I stand to take in the full glory of the moment, loose arms dangling by my side.

He seems confused by my grin.

'What's that for? Cayenne?' His face traces back over words we may have spoken, actions that may have warranted such a violent reprisal.

I can't stop myself grinning at his stupid face and bare chest covered in grey hair. I walk out, leaving him rubbing at his skull where the tin has left a small dent. I make a note to serve him beans on toast from the offending can.

When I think about who deserves what and when, there really is no reason to it at all. Do some women deserve children more than I? Do others feel the same crushing emptiness inside when month after month the ache of their period leaks the dream of motherhood away? I try to remember at what age it switched up a gear from yearning to desperation. That ticking body clock like an unwanted tune in my ear tapping out the rhythm of words, not-this-time, not-this-time, not-this-time. I'd make deals with the spirits, the angels, God, Jesus, the saints, any unseen helper who could potentially help manifest a baby inside my womb. I even plead with the devil: he was an angel once, after all. He knew what it was like to be down on his luck, cast out by his beloved family.

I slop the baked beans into a saucepan and turn up the heat.

MYRRH

'Are you walking home, Myrrh?' Daniel slipped his bag over his shoulder as he followed her out the door. The shift had finished with minor drama, an easy day of the usual routine. Though those days always seemed to drag more.

They emerged from the stuffy interior of the care home into the smooth heat of the afternoon. Summer always made Myrrh more sociable; it opened her up like the wide leaves of a sycamore tree.

Daniel had a lightness about him. Most of the residents asked after him when he wasn't there. He offered Myrrh a sweet from a white paper bag.

'Pear drops!' She took a red one and popped it into her mouth. The scratchy sugar coating felt good against the roof of her mouth. 'These used to be my favourites when I was little.'

'Mine too.' He grinned. 'We used to spend all our pocket money on sweets and comics.'

'We had the best sweet shop in our village.' She told him about Alice and school.

'You grew up near here?'

'Yeah, my parents still live in the same house I grew up in.' Myrrh felt shy telling him this.

'Must be nice having them nearby.' Daniel crunched loudly on his sweet.

'It is. Where do your parents live?'

'They split up when I was a kid. Dad's in London. Mum moved to Cornwall.'

'That's where my mum lives – I mean lived.'

'I thought you said they lived here.' He gave her a puzzled look.

'My birth mother is in Cornwall – was in Cornwall. I don't know anymore.' She hated using that term.

Birth and *mother* meant so many things. When she spoke those words they were loaded with uncertainty.

'I didn't know you were adopted.' The way he spoke made her feel safe, and she noticed how much lighter she felt as she walked back to her house. People can smile all the time but not feel happy. She knew that because she was one of those people; she covered up her discomfort with a smile. But when someone really makes you smile, you remember it and, you can feel it in all your body not just your lips or cheeks.

The cat shot out as Myrrh opened the door and ran through the gap in the hedge towards the neighbour's driveway.

'Whoa tiger!' Daniel stepped back to let him pass.

'He likes to pretend he rules the neighbourhood, but actually he loves a cuddle.' Myrrh was rambling. 'Would you like to come in for a cup of tea or some elderflower cordial – homemade?' Her mouth felt sticky from the pear drops.

She was pleased with how the garden had blossomed. All the flowers had exploded in colourful bursts, marigolds campaigning with the showy petals of pansies and the leafy shrubs that she'd inherited from the previous owner. They sank onto the cool lawn, thankful for the light breeze coming in off the coast. It was a dreamy day when time seemed to slide and linger like the haze of heat over the town.

'How did you find out about your mum? Your birth mother?' Lying on his side and propped up on one arm, Daniel sipped his elderflower.

'I've got some paperwork. All I've done so far is send a letter to an old address.'

'And?'

'And nothing.'

She couldn't bring herself to mention the failed trip to Cornwall. How empty the house there seemed. How she felt like a stalker just being there.

'So what are you going to do now?'

'What can I do?' She couldn't force her birth mother to reply, and wasn't even sure her letter had been read by who she wanted to read it. It might just be another dead end instead of a start. What had begun with a clear purpose – to find where she had come from – seemed inconceivably naïve when faced with the possibility that she might not find the truth, and somewhere in the recesses of her mind she anticipated that those she sought might not want to be found.

Women were offered anonymity when they relinquished their babies in the 1970s: perhaps they found that reassuring in some way, to be told that they could be found only if their child decided to instigate the search by digging up the papers. They were told that their baby had gone to a good home, been placed in the care of a new complete family, convinced it was for baby's best interests, and they signed them away. Yet the birth mother's name was still recorded on the birth certificate like some scribble in the marginalia of life.

'I can't imagine not knowing my family,' Daniel said.

Myrrh cut him short. 'I have a family.'

'Yes, what I mean is I know my great-grandfather worked on the railways and kept chickens. I know that my father has a birthmark on his leg in exactly the same place as his father. I know that my grandfather used to say it was a bullet wound, but it wasn't really. My dad said I inherited Grandad's chin.' He jutted it out towards her and stopped his ramble abruptly to laugh with her.

'Do you think having that link matters?'

Myrrh thought about Enid from the care home. There was no way of verifying what they said was true or not, but Enid once told her she'd had a child when she was fifteen. She said they had tricked her into giving her baby away. Myrrh asked what happened to him, but Enid just smiled a sad, thin smile. There was no record, no paperwork from that time; it would've been like searching through the sand on a beach for a grain of salt when the tide had washed in and out for years. *At least I have names and dates*, Myrrh thought, *and an address*.

The cat bounded into the living room. He sat in the doorway and posed like a porcelain statue then prowled toward Daniel, purring and brushing up against his legs.

'He likes you.'

Daniel reached down to stroke him and was nudged affectionately. 'You're strong, aren't you?'

'You should see him when he wants food.'

'I'd better be off.' Daniel, sensing their time together was at a close, stepped outside and the cat bounded after him.

She waved and probably shut the door a little too abruptly before sifting through the stack of post to retrieve a small white envelope that caught her eye. Handwritten post was so rare these days: there was something intensely nostalgic about it. She turned it over and stared at the postmark. Before she opened it, she already knew where it was from.

CAYENNE

Do they do it on purpose? Those smug bitches with their offspring and all the trailing paraphernalia that comes with motherhood. They wear it like a sash draped over their dripping bosoms. I can smell them as they come closer, milky sour and vaginal. How easy it seems for them to grow this other being inside their body and carry on moving in the world, harvesting another parasite to suckle, another dribbling brat to brainwash with their own fuckery, with their own inadequacies. Selfish sluts. Some already have two, three, four kids and still they greedily have another when other women, like me, have none.

MYRRH

Myrrh was ten years old when she first ran away from home. She packed a bag of essentials: a bag of crisps, a cereal bar, a change of underwear and her dad's spare penknife. She had the romantic notion that she could survive alone, that the fairy folk would take her in; she'd pick the berries and subsist off the bounty that was in front of her. A couple of dog walkers nodded a greeting as she tramped across the fields pretending to know which direction she was heading. But the ground was uneven, and her socks began to rub on her heels, the start of a blister creating a nagging discomfort each time she took a step.

After scuffing about by the hedgerows and listening to the birds, all hope of finding somewhere warm and dry to sleep for the night retreated. She thought of her bed and its clean, dry sheets, and of her mum tucking her in and giving her a kiss. The crisps and cereal bar were eaten up almost minutes into her journey, and her belly began to rumble. Everything started to look so spiky and unwelcoming. What should have been a beautiful bright scene turned misty grey and heavy. Then, as if the fields knew she did not belong there, the world turned hostile and alien. The harsh cawing of rooks in the distance seemed to predict the onset of clouds that soon shrouded

the late summer sun. A blackbird chattered past her into the
hedge, making her stumble, her heart racing. A sheep in the
distance let out a low bleat, like an old, drunk man heckling
her. What she had planned to be her new start as an earth pixie,
an expedition where she would transform into another being,
became muddied and dank.

She looked around for something to drink. The rhyne at the
edge of the drove was clogged with black silt, the water flow
impeded by discarded drinks cans and plastic food wrappers. It
smelt of old curtains, moulded up behind thin dirty windows.
Her mouth felt claggy and dry; she had not thought about
her need for water. Around her the ditches lining the fields
were designed to fill with rain, but even if she attempted to
scramble down between the brambles, it looked stagnant and
undrinkable. It had been a hot summer, but rain had still
collected in the ruts carved out by the cattle and livestock, yet
it pooled in dark brown effluent. Buzzing insects and biting
flies pitched on her clammy arms and wouldn't leave her alone.
She was tired from walking yet had probably only travelled a
quarter of a mile from her house when she decided running
away from home was a bad idea after all. What was she running
from anyhow?

this way
no, this way
follow the breadcrumbs
lost little girl
no one will miss you

Goblin chuckled and goaded her to take the path where the
brambles had grown thick and sharp, nettles higher than her waist
ready to brush against her bare legs. It was too uncomfortable, too
lonely to carry on.

A knotted root tripped her up, and she felt the rush of pain
shoot up from her knee. When she inspected the skin it was pitted

with gravel and dirt, small flecks of blood blooming like buds. As she sat in the undergrowth she noticed insects buzz around not even noticing her, as if she was too insignificant to be seen, even by something much smaller than herself.

She felt a familiar churning inside and braced herself for the goblin to make her feel worse. He knew her weaknesses, tripped her up at every available opportunity.

run home to mummy
oh wait
not your mummy
no one wants someone's stained goods
some other mother's cast-offs

He was trying to crawl out of her throat, ripping up her neck so hot tears spilled down her cheeks. She swallowed him back down and struggled to her feet, rushing along through the nettles, not even flinching as they stung her over and over in hot sharp stabs across her calves and shins.

When she returned, expecting there to be mayhem from her unexpected disappearance, her mum was still on her hands and knees gardening and her dad was in his shed, sorting tools and bits of wood.

they never missed you
you may as well be invisible

No matter how hard she tried to run away from the goblin, it tapped into her weak spot.

'What have you done to your legs?' Her mum gestured to the red scratches and angry welts where the nettles had stung her. Myrrh shrugged and went inside.

Her attempt at finding a new life was short-lived and, reflecting back on that time, she realised that was one of many moments when what she was really searching for was solitude or time to contemplate. There was no need for her to go to such extremes. She was searching outside herself when the answers were inside, fiercely guarded by the goblin.

Her mum had received a letter from an old neighbour from way back, an epistle of her annual illnesses listed in chronological order. *Arrhythmia. Eczema. Haemorrhoids. Hypertension.* Myrrh had looked up hypertension in the dictionary and was disappointed.

Later that evening as the sun dipped behind the low hills, her mum asked if she'd like to walk with her to the post box on the corner, but she retreated to her bedroom and watched from her window as her mum passed the stone wall that edged the front garden and disappeared from sight.

CAYENNE

A woman in the post office was chattering away to me in the queue. I tried to zone her out but she wouldn't shut up talking about Frances this, Frances that, who was going to study music, and Graham who had joined the navy, twins but couldn't be more different.

'They always need us, don't they?' She rolled her eyes but I could see the pride bursting out of her.

I said nothing. But I could sense the way she looked at me differently, taking in the roundness of my belly, the way I was rubbing the small of my back. It was a risk but I was willing to take it.

'When's it due?' She smiled.

'I've got a while yet.' I smiled back at her and could feel the heat rising in my cheeks.

'Would you prefer a boy or girl?'

'We're just thrilled as long as they are healthy.' My cheeks were starting to ache as I held the fixed smile.

'Well, enjoy the peace while it lasts.' She turned to face the front of the queue and do her business.

I let my cheeks drop now she no longer faced me.

When I got back in the car, I unfastened the cushion from around my waist and flung it on the back seat. This charade is tiresome but it is necessary if I am to lead my new life without suspicion.

MARIAN

She carries her story like a card in her pocket. It rests, the edges curling with the movement and shifting of her body. For now, it is separated from the pack, but will soon be rediscovered.

Here is Marian's story.

One of secrets.

She does not know how she has become the grey-haired woman who faces her in the mirror each morning. At times this does not bother her, and at times she hides behind a smile. She appears content in her not-knowing state and then doubts her reasoning.

With some reticence, she had agreed to have a tarot reading, a treat from her friend. She thought it would only confirm how useless others' advice often turns out to be. The woman doing the reading was disappointingly ordinary, wearing jeans and an old sweater, and made her feel so welcome that she felt guilty for judging her before they met. She gave Marian a look, reminding her of the nurses at the hospital all those years ago.

The cards were dealt in a pattern shaped like a cross and told her things no one else could have possibly known. Children and family were at the forefront of the reading though she had said nothing to hint at her past. A revelation of sorts.

'A secret. Something lost.' The card reader paused before moving on to tell her that she needed to take care of her health, to release the burden of thoughts that kept her awake at night, to not worry so much about the things she could not change.

It was not as if she wanted to keep that distant part of her life secret, but she felt so out of control when she found out she was pregnant that the best option was to deal with it alone. She had discovered it in a toilet at work, of all places, and felt foolish at not realising sooner: the weight gain, her sudden dips in mood and an intense desire for sweet things. When she was pregnant with her son five years earlier, it had been pickled onions – in fact, anything doused in vinegar. By the time she realised, it was too late to do anything about it. The father of her unborn child had disappeared from her insular life. He had made it clear there was no serious relationship. Never had been. In some small way she was relieved that he was not close by to cross her path or interfere in what ultimately became her decision.

She had panicked when the realisation first came to light, and wanted to call someone but didn't know who. So she ignored it, knowing it would not go away, wishing it might sort itself out. Her mother was dead before she could form memories of her. Her father died in an accident at work. She was raised by her grandfather, who did not discuss women's issues.

It was a shock for her to find out the horrors of menstruation on her own, bundling paper towels between her legs every month until a kindly teacher asked her if she'd like to try something 'a little easier'. There seemed such shame that she felt cursed by anything womanly. Then she met a man, married, gave birth to their son. But she left him. There was no catalytic reason, just a parting of ways, like the worn seams of an old sweater.

She thought a friend who had gone through the initiation of childbirth might understand her predicament and the complexities of it all. But her brain nagged at her to keep it secret. The fewer people who knew, the better. Her separated husband was still in contact for her son's sake, but after she moved to Cornwall with its solid rocks and fierce waves, the fresh start was not as fresh as she imagined it would be. It was as if sadness had followed her, and a change in location did not remove that feeling.

The urgent need to share the knowledge of her unplanned pregnancy with another soul was replaced by ways she could conceal her growing belly from work colleagues. How stupid it all seemed now: the impulsive urgency of those passionate meetings and partings, whispering so her son, asleep in the next room, would not hear them. Had he promised her anything? If it weren't for the pregnancy, she may have left that period of her life behind, the hazy memory of an old flame with little significance. He had moved on; she had remained, like the enduring crash of waves against the coastline.

She rarely planned anything. Even the move, the separation from her husband, was spontaneous and chaotic. The little Cornish cottage was a mess when she arrived on the doorstep, and its old dirt stuck fast, like doubt, to the floors, walls and ceilings. She spent a month scrubbing and rinsing away the grime before it was in any fit state to receive visitors. She lived in one room at a time, shifting belongings in bags that she stacked in corners so there was space to sit or eat, or for her son to play.

Her work colleagues were a fun antidote to the mess of her home life. That's where she had met him; he was educated, exotic, and like no man she had ever met before. A world away from her husband.

But when she found out she was carrying the child of this enigmatic man, a monologue of questions arose in her head. And the resounding answer to them all was 'wait'.

It all seemed so shameful, so shabby. She was afraid the gossip about her would spread like oil. She had tough decisions to make, and she had to make them alone.

MYRRH

She dreamed of a solitary bee dying on a pavement, legs pathetically pedalling the air.

When she woke it was still dark, and the cat groaned where he slept at the foot of the bed as she shifted her legs under the duvet. The radio clicked on mid-sentence: 'Do you mean to say humans are intrinsically selfish?'

'What I mean is, we have lost our animal instincts; we are the least authentic of all species. We are fake.'

'Bit heavy for seven-fifteen on Tuesday morning.' Laughter. Traffic news, lorry broken down on the A37, tailbacks, not helped by wet roads, shorter days, dark evenings, soggy leaves.

At least we don't eat our own young, thought Myrrh, *or do we? In our own sly way, swallowing them up like a witch in a folk tale, coating them with the internal messes of our own lives and spewing them back out to deal with the afterbirth.*

Everything seemed grey at this time of year. The sky seemed to be in mourning for another lost season.

Myrrh turned on her phone expecting a barrage of messages, but most were updates from her mum, who missed her terribly. Had Myrrh missed anyone, ever? She was expert at fitting into her community wherever she landed in life. Those were her family for that time, however brief. The brothers and sisters she never grew up with, the father figures who had come and gone, the mothers of others: they all played their part.

She found similarities and differences in their mannerisms, picked them out like sifting through coloured pebbles or coins. Anything that had a noticeable connection was plucked out of the meaningless to try to make sense of the melee in her head: how people held their knives and forks, the way they drank tea, facial expressions, accents, sayings, the shape of noses, the distance between eyes, lips, hand gestures, height, body shape, feet, heads, brains, hearts, eyes, tears.

The shit that people talked about – the utter, mindless shit that spilled forth from their mouths.

lies, all lies

CAYENNE

I am not unrealistic. I do have feelings and understand that it must be hard for his daughter too. She was so used to being the centre of attention before my arrival on the scene. Then I moved in and upset the apple cart. Hostility moved in alongside me.

Yet, as he says, she has her own life. She comes and goes and has not mastered the art of stillness. Or discernment. Or respectfulness. Shallow bitch. For me to be aware of her shallowness is useful. For example, she is easily impressed by financial wealth and material success. For her, this seems to be the ultimate goal. Regularly citing friends or acquaintances with large houses, expensive possessions, new cars... It is not the value system I've ever aspired to or ever will. We disagree, and while she thinks she's right, I know she is not.

Besides, she's not my child. I want a baby, not some fully grown monster filled with another couple's weaknesses.

I think I know where I will get one.

MARIAN

Her movements are like a spider, re-mending a web, methodically starting over. *This is just how it is*, she thought. *The way of the world.* A child was born, a fate decided.

There may have been a seed of hope at one time that the enigmatic stranger she had grown fond of could have been a father in the true present sense, but as the pregnancy progressed, she felt leaps of dread in her belly that may have been a quickening of the baby, or may just easily have been intuition of what was to come.

He had gone.

Left town and made a new life up country. The talk of staying in touch was flimsy and non-committal, but she realised now it was a kinder way for him to say goodbye, to detach from the threads of a former life when, in fact, he turned the corner and severed all ties.

Some threads, she thought, *have a habit of attaching themselves unseen, only visible when the cold light of day catches them.*

In those last uncomfortable days before the baby was born, Marian still had to assign her thoughts to decisions and meetings with social workers, and plans for the baby once it exited the confines of her body. She was resolute, then she was undecided, then she was overcome with certainty. She could not care for it even in the interim. She had to sever ties, just like he had done with her. They asked her in that tender, head-tilting way: could she perhaps nurse the baby, just for its first few weeks until the paperwork was finalised? She said 'no' thirteen times in one meeting.

Two days after, a change in the temperature, when sticky heat made lizards run up the walls. Her waters broke as she was walking back from the bus stop. Love was mentioned in nearly every song when she switched on the wireless, an ironic poke at her lack of that elusive emotion. How could she forget this? Love may as well have punched her in the guts over and over. Love did not make the baby she had given up; love did not bind her to its father; love did not even save the day. Love was dead and buried as far as she was concerned.

CAYENNE

Hubble bubble toil and trouble. Oh, for fuck's sake. Am I supposed to be the witch? The wicked stepmother? What am I if I can't even reproduce? What worth do I have in society if I don't raise a child? My own child. Answer me that question. Am I selfish to want what other women just take for granted?

Bring back that young girl's lungs and liver for me to feast upon. You know what you have created. Let me ingest all the goodness so I can imbibe youth's beauty. I'll gorge on her innards until I'm full of fecundity. Fill me up. Let me grow fat.

I pull the case out from beside the wardrobe and open it. I have placed my passport alongside the clean, neat piles of baby clothes and nappies. I press my face against the soft fabric and breathe hungry breaths.

MARIAN

In those long days that followed the birth, she had few visitors to the cottage. A neighbour brought milk and bread, made her cups of tea, chatted about the weather and Robert Plant – some singer in a band who had been in a car crash in Greece – and said that Haile Selassie had died. These well-wishers rambled on about others' lives but didn't directly ask how *hers* was. Their kindness was more by indirect gesture of providing something to eat; food seemed a natural way of reaching out in this time of loss. Because it was a mourning of sorts, a silent unspoken grief.

She had not painted much during the pregnancy. Creativity had dried up, like her appetite. As though the baby had taken all the creative power she had, or buried it so far inside her there was no conceivable way of extracting it again.

A colleague from work visited during the weeks that followed, and Marian felt more at ease when he was around, his presence lifting a sorrowful veil. He sat with her and gave her mundane updates from the hospital. A patient had brought in flowers for the nurses after her hip operation; a ward sister had told off the new orderly for taking too many smoking breaks. He didn't mention the vacancy her baby had left, but said she looked well.

———————

The nights were the worst, when the trees sounded like the lonely whispers of the sea outside her windows.

She felt the urge to paint. A renewed passion.

She carefully steered a heavy box of magazines, kept for future reference, off a wooden settle seat and lifted the lid. There were her paints and paper, where she had stored them all those years ago.

A sheet of paper was wedged down the side of the box. Marian carefully dislodged it and stared at the muted arc of a rainbow above a field. An early watercolour, rushed in composition but very familiar. She had painted it the Easter following the birth. Rainbows, she had been told, were a good sign. They carried the hint of a promise in their complete spectrum of colours.

She recalled days when she would paint without heed to time or routine; peaceful interludes where she was a conduit for all the colours surging within her. She tried to recall when that harmony had been so eroded, when she had lost her urge to create something new. Her paints and brush were a partnership that worked as one, each needing the other. A line from a curious collection of quotations flashed up before her, *'Temperance restored me and I welcomed its powerful elixir, for I was soon to come eye to eye with the Devil.'* She shivered and placed the painting back in the box and closed the lid.

CAYENNE

He moans about the noise of the fan at night but it is so hot without it. Even with all the windows open, the heat layers upon itself like syrup in a jar. When I cannot sleep, I stand in the garden at night letting my feet sink into the cool grass. I think of how dependent I am on this man who has invited me to live in his home. I am writing an inventory of what I own: clothes, a gold ring, some books, my case of new baby clothes. I am virtually a pauper. If I disappeared there would be nothing left to show I had existed. Nothing at all.

By midday the next day we've not spoken one word to each other. He is due to go out this evening and won't be back until after dark – after midnight. I'm used to him doing as he pleases, with his routines I've had to fit around my life. I need to hold on a while longer. I need to stick to my plan.

Do I believe him when he has said in the past, *I love you more than I've ever loved anyone*? No, I do not. I am extremely upset that he cannot understand how difficult it is for me and his only response is to say, 'I can't help that she's my daughter'. I am not part of his family.

I never will be part of his family.

It is up to me to create my own.

MYRRH

Her brother was the only person she knew who turned the light off when he entered the room, reverse-announcing his arrival. Dim the lights, draw the curtains, retreat into darkness. It was an annoying habit, and most annoying when she was in the room reading or sitting or sewing.

'Sorry, Myrrh.' He'd flick the switch so the light returned. 'Didn't see you there.'

you're invisible
a nobody
nothing

When they were growing up together, she thought these annoying behaviours were a way to trigger an argument, but he had loads of habits. They couldn't all be to annoy her. The rush of cold water hitting the metal basin hissed in her ears, on, then off, then on. Six times until he'd filled a glass and slurped it down. Water galloping down his gullet made her want to throttle him. She turned her nose up at him wiping his mouth with his sleeve. She'd tut as the thump of the glass by the side of the sink ricocheted off her eardrums.

She'd fuel the hate into feeding her goblin as each crumb of leftover food staring back at her, each floundering dirtied knife on a greasy worktop, or each discarded piece of clothing became part of her arsenal.

useless
unseen
don't care

Her room had order in the neat rows of books, a glass cabinet of china-headed dolls in national costume, a chair with a neatly centred heart-shaped cushion, a pot for her pens and pencils, and a wardrobe whose door didn't bulge from overstuffing.

don't touch my stuff
keep out
shut it out

Their shared space was the playroom downstairs, the place friends could hang out, though they rarely played together as siblings. She or her brother might make an appearance if the other's friend was visiting, just to mark their territory or be included in some way.

The dartboard, the mini pool table, the record player, the Commodore 64 computer, his Action Men, his Transformers, his toy soldiers, his Lego, his toy cars.

his, all his
you're only second best
afterthought

Some books, a few dollies, a miniature shop with edible coloured popped rice to substitute as foodstuffs and grey plastic coins to trade items.

second hand like you
discarded
someone else's rubbish

Action Man invaded the territory of her doll's house. Even when he was discarded on the floor, his eagle eyes still shiftily looked up at her.

I'm watching you
you don't belong here
he does, he's better

Sindy went missing. She was discovered several weeks later sitting brazenly on the spongy terracotta-striped sofa, sporting a green mohican. Myrrh could not believe her eyes. She knew immediately her brother had instigated revenge with *her* coloured felt-tip pens, which had been left strewn on the carpet, the green pen conspicuously lidless, the ink dried out.

revenge
sweet revenge
spin the wheel
roll the dice

There was shouting (their father) and door slamming (her brother) and a silent frowning dinner during which everyone was forced into passive-aggressive dish-passing of peas and potatoes with pursed lips (their mother) and chewing slowly, occasionally clearing a throat or scraping a chair back to fetch a glass of water. Myrrh kept her eyes on her plate, not wanting to look at her brother. She gripped her knife. A chicken leg stared up at her from her plate.

plunge it in
twist it
break the bones

She wanted to plunge her knife through the greasy meat, splintering the bone and cracking the plate.

I'm watching you
I know all the things you do
your dirty little secrets
dirty little secret

Board games filling the cupboards, boxes loaded with arms and legs and torsos, games with blue/red/yellow/green buttons that attempted to answer unanswerable questions such as *where are they?* Or *will I find them?*

CAYENNE

My body is made of waterfalls and lush foliage. I am soft moss on smooth stone. Everything about me glistens. Fresh air fills me. I'm free. My body is healthy, with youthful vigour. I can feel the fullness of my thighs, my breasts. All my scars have disappeared, the seen and unseen ones. I feel stronger than I've ever felt and all because of him.

He is here with me, my angel, my ghost lover. Colours merge and flow with his promises. *All this*, he says, *and more*. Forests and castles spring up around us, blue sky stretching into the forever after, the great wide-open space of oceans lies beyond the bright snow-capped mountains. *It's all yours*, he says, and beckons me to follow him.

It all makes sense. When things fit together there are no questions of it being right. *You deserve this*, he tells me. *All of this and more*. I look out across the fields, ripe and abundant with fruits and grain. Butterflies land on multi-coloured blooms, and birds soar across a turquoise sky dotted with delicate white clouds.

I am leaning against the bark of a strong oak tree as I sit beneath its shade, at my feet a Moses basket. *All yours*, he says. And I reach forward to peek beneath the blanket, my hand inches from what lies inside. I notice the unblemished skin of my hands, my own but a young woman's hands now. *All you've ever dreamed of,* he says. *All yours.*

All mine.

CAYENNE

Of course, there had to be a ceremony around the announcement. Of course, there had to be something dramatic to mark the occasion. Of course, we all had to witness it. I cannot even bring myself to utter the words aloud.

She is pregnant.

The BITCH is pregnant.

My dreams and nightmares have arrived at once. I wanted a baby in this house. But it is not to be mine.

Her father is livid. He cannot even begin to look at her for the shame it brings him. I can tell by the set of his jawline that no matter how much he loves her, he cannot bend to her will this time. The baby must go and we must never speak of it in this house. It is an embarrassing stain on his reputation.

Maybe I can convince him that this is a blessing. After all, this could be our child.

MYRRH

They were solar systems apart, hopelessly separated, not even sharing one iota of DNA. His white-blond hair, her dark thick waves, his pale blue eyes, her dark green irises, his skin turning pink with the slightest sunshine, hers bronzing like a statue, his shape so unlike hers, his face, her face, and on and on and so forth and so forth. Yet they were raised as brother and sister, so that was what they were. Siblings. That was their link, and love resided somewhere in that messy mixture they inhabited together.

lost

sad losers

Myrrh knew her brother had got off with a few of the older girls although he never had a steady girlfriend, but there were a few who thought they were, and it was Myrrh who bore the brunt of the fallout.

Kay Pierce was one such jilted party. She'd make snide remarks and try to whack Myrrh with her bag as she stomped to the back of the school bus. She always wore make-up: thick gloopy eyelashes and sticky lip gloss that shimmered as she chewed gum, which she'd poke her tongue through before resuming her incessant chomping. She had a resting bitch face and she was a known bully.

you deserve it

no one likes you
not even your fake brother

Myrrh resolved to have it out once and for all with Kay Pierce one day on the journey home from school. She waited nervously all day, rehearsing her words as though she was in a play, pausing for effect but not too long for fear she'd be ignored, or Kay would interject. She read Judy Blume in the library and tried to channel some inner bravado. The bus filled, and Myrrh made sure she got on first so Kay would have to walk past her seat so she could catch her eye.

catch her eye
pop it between your teeth
squeeze until it bursts

Myrrh watched as Kay approached.

trip her up
stick out your fat foot

She was getting closer, popping her gum through her tongue and sashaying up the aisle. Myrrh felt inside her pencil case for her compass. She held the sharp point poking out.

stab her
make her bleed

Kay was two seats away and had spotted Myrrh. A smirk spreading across her face.

lash out
do it NOW

Kay popped her gum, grabbing the back of Myrrh's seat as she swept by.

stab her hard

Myrrh gripped the compass but couldn't move. The bitch had got away with it. Her one chance had been missed.

worthless

swallow it down
chew on it
The goblin was right. She didn't deserve a place in this family.

CAYENNE

She cries all the time now. He has told her that there is no way she can keep the baby. People will talk. *It's enough that we are living here all together. But a baby in the house would not be practical.* I burn inside when he says these words. What if I were the mother? What if the baby could be ours instead? What if the baby is mine? There's no way she would allow this, not that she has any power in this situation. Her father will give her an ultimatum: you keep the baby and never grace this doorway again, or you go on a little holiday, have the baby, and return without it.

My ghost lover whispers in my ear most nights. *All mine,* he says, *all mine.* I see the fear in her eyes and try to fight my urge to grab her and run. I will bide my time.

That's all you can do when waiting for something to emerge, to grow nearer to you.

MYRRH

Myrrh woke with a dream still clinging to her. The Emperor from the tarot deck held an emerald lens suspended on a golden chain, and she could see a scene in the reflection.

His measure lies in the eyes of his subjects who do not smile, who shuffle in rags, who die before their lives are fully spent for there is nothing to live for. They do not look up; their gaze is directed towards the dirt-scraped paths beneath their feet. For the ones ruled by a tyrant share his emptiness; what he holds inside himself is played out in his subject's daily lives. He does not know what his heart is for.

Through the lens she saw herself meeting a man considerably older than she was. She was talking to him and recognised him as someone who was no longer in her life, no longer important. She watched as she became fascinated by what he was saying. She saw this version of herself believing his silky words.

The gold, the silver, the ornaments, lacquered boxes of stolen jewels from the hearts of his knights, diamonds from the tears of the lost children, mountains of treasure, hoards of coins, barrels of fine wine, storerooms of food, castles and forts, arsenals, fleets, armies, armaments, ramparts, ensigns, spears, bounty that would last for more than ten lifetimes. All this is nothing when ruled by him.

She saw a woman's heart. Small and black and hampered with small darts, as if tiny daggers had lodged there and become putrefied. She couldn't see the woman's face, but areas of her body had become transparent; crawling insects nested in her groin where they laid larvae that mutated into slithering, centipedal creatures. She saw light flicker and fade with each moment, while this infected heart pumped harder and the black creatures enlarged as if pulsating with the host's life blood. From the mists a sword appeared and sliced the heart in half. The woman crumbled to the ground, and a creature rose up from her chest with wings and hooves and a misshapen head like that of a horse.

CAYENNE

She won't tell us who the father is, though she must know. Why the secrecy? She is so young but old enough to bear a child. She has no shame that she is single, unmarried, certain of the fact her father will somehow sort this 'little problem' out. He has a pained look in his eye, like a dog that has been beaten by its owner. His first grandchild will be a bastard. I can tell he is processing this behind a façade of pride. I cannot eat a thing. I feel sick all the time thinking of the unfairness of it all. It is all so unhip.

'Is there a way we can make this work?' I know if I speak to him in bed at least he cannot walk away from me.

'How can it work?' he asks.

'We could say it's ours, mine.' I stroke his cheek with my hand.

'What are you saying?' He catches my hand.

'The baby,' I say. 'It could be our child.'

'Our child? How?'

'We could say it's mine.' I look at him, pleading that he will say yes.

MYRRH

She walked a different route to the seafront that day, cutting across the edge of the golf course and up over the sand dunes. The tide was out, slicked back, as far as she could see to the smooth mound of Stert Island dotted with wading birds, and beyond that, mudflats framing the ponderous Bristol Channel. It was Mediterranean hot, and people had spread themselves over the sand, marking their territory with striped windbreaks and blankets. Several adults and children were playing football, with plastic buckets, spades and discarded clothing for goalposts. Myrrh walked past them. Near to her, a baby started squalling and waving its legs like a stranded crab on a blanket. No one comforting her. No one taking any notice. Who had comforted Myrrh in those first few lonely weeks? She stood, watching the baby. Watching it cry.

bad baby
all alone
damaged goods
just like you

This baby appeared all alone, but in truth they were surrounded by others who took no notice of them. In unison with its cries a siren, high pitched and close, wheeled past along the sea front. An ambulance. She caught a glimpse of its blue flashing light as she reached the pier.

Picking up her pace, she walked towards the concrete steps that led up to the pavement. By the time she had reached the road, the ambulance was pulling away. People were milling about, turning to watch it leave. A woman leaned on the sea wall clutching a bag, scanning passers-by. Myrrh turned her back on the sea and scanned from right to left, the nerves rippling in her belly.

Twisting their heads to show beady black eyes seagulls circled like sharks above the heads of a couple eating ice cream. Myrrh walked to the front of the lifeboat station, a small building, but all she saw was a family packing away sandy towels and shoes into the boot of their car. Music pumped from a car stereo as it patrolled along the seafront, and a mobility scooter decorated with Yorkshire terrier stickers shot past on the pavement, a dog, perfectly matching the stickers, perched like a totem in the basket at the front.

She tried to match up the parts she knew about the start of her life but Goblin kept jumbling them up, reordering, shredding the evidence into such tiny incomprehensible pieces that it would be impossible to make sense of it.

Mother. Father. Birth. Foster home. Paperwork. Decisions. Others. Adopted. A timeline of events with nothing to hold on to. Avenues she wanted to explore that led nowhere. Brick wall. Brick wall. Brick wall.

nobody wants a bad baby
caul-smeared
the water is there
walk in
swallow it
swallow the ocean

Right now she felt like she was drowning in the sludge of her own making. Surely it was time for someone to lift her out of the murky water, to resuscitate her and stroke her wet hair saying, 'Everything's okay. Everything will be okay.' Someone who had the answers she was looking for. Someone to tell her the most important thing of all. Who she was.

But that was when the goblin would pirouette in circles up and down her spinal cord.

they'll never tell
you'll never know
name me
name me
go on, dare you

And Myrrh would retreat into herself. Into silence. And Goblin would laugh.

I win, I win
you lose, you lose

CAYENNE

Where is my ghost lover? Each night I wait for him. I force myself to sleep so he can visit me. I am restless and wake many times. But nothing. Not even dreams, not even a glimmer of fantasy. I wake in the mornings feeling sick.

Has he abandoned me?

I'm finding it more and more difficult to remember my dreams. Is it because I'm sleeping next to a broken man who's embarrassed by his daughter's actions?

This morning I felt the bubbling of frustration surface again, his grieving over something that should be a celebration. It triggered in me some anger. I was annoyed somehow by his inadequacy. Why must women always mop up the mess?

MYRRH

Myrrh stared at the email she had written. No matter how long she looked at the words she couldn't quite place herself in the recipient's shoes. How would she feel if she received this message? Disbelieving, excited, angry, confused?

This may come as a bit of a shock... I think we share the same father...

Maybe she shouldn't have been surprised about the lack of reaction to her earlier letter. Decades had passed. People made their own lives, moved on. But the consequences of their actions remained. A knot of resentment tightened inside her. What kind of life had he lived with no thought directed towards her, his daughter? A life raising his other children, forming bonds with them and then refusing to even acknowledging her existence.

...a bit of a shock...

What about the shock of finding out you were not wanted as a baby? She had had to deal with that her whole life. Goblin rat-a-tat-tatted against her bones.

who are you?
where are you from?
useless piece of shit
no one cares about you
no one ever did

It wasn't difficult to find what she needed on the internet. Just as when she found her birth father, she entered a few carefully worded searches and his name popped up again. Social-media profiles were mostly locked down now. She couldn't message him. He knew she was trying. But then, under his list of friends on Facebook, she saw something. Sons. With the same surname, they had to be. If he wouldn't respond to her she would at least make those closest to him know that she existed.

name me

go on

dare you

She'd been denied that right for too long. Didn't everyone deserve to know where they came from?

name me

Goblin played the same tune against her ribs. He was angry, she could tell. If she wasn't careful, he could break out of there, smash his way through her skin and bone and muscle. She always worried about what would happen if that was ever to occur.

All those years ago when she felt she never fit with the name her adoptive parents had given her. Myrrh. A joke of a name really: when she was a child her parents nicknamed her Myrrh. It was supposed to be affectionate. A result of a strange quirk of speech, her way of mumbling, of murmuring…

Murmur.

Myrrh-Myrrh.

Even as a baby she would utter sounds that seemed otherworldly, murmurings. So it was Myrrh that settled with her.

She read the email through one final time and pressed *Send*.

CAYENNE

He holds up an empty jar of piccalilli as I lie in bed, non-verbally gesturing that the end of the world will almost certainly happen if the store cupboard is not replenished by his next meal. I think resentfully of all the things I have to compromise on. If I weren't to do it, it would not be done: arrangements to find his daughter somewhere to stay until she has the baby, directions, travel, housework and social-services meetings, not to mention all the other things he seems to think just happen such as shopping, cooking, cleaning, breathing.

My left hip is twinging with a sharp pain down my leg. I am trapped by the passing of time. I make up scenarios where he brings me flowers, takes me out for a meal.

What sort of man is he?

He needs to be careful, especially now he needs help dealing with his daughter's little problem.

MYRRH

Dolls in national dress; thimbles, postcards, soap, trinkets, pebbles, dried pressed flowers, pigs, donkeys, frogs, stickers: all these things she would hoard and squirrel away in her bedroom in boxes under the bed, on shelves, on the bedside table. Her dad built a cabinet with a glass front to mount on the wall where she could place all her dolls, some unopened in their plastic cylinders. These dust-gathering collections were rarely looked at once they had been acquired. But Myrrh knew she owned them – they were hers and hers alone – and God help anyone who touched them or disturbed them in anyway.

Her heart was beating so hard she was sure everyone else could hear it. The urgency to ask her mum about the time before her birth pressed against her ribcage, but when she arrived at her parents' house she sensed it wasn't the right time.

'Mum?' Just the sound of Myrrh's voice made her mum's face crumple into unbearable sorrow.

Robbie hadn't even been driving very fast. Her mum held her arms out. Myrrh couldn't speak so let her mum sob and she sobbed, too, in constrained heart-wrenching gasps, like a coil of rope or a boa constrictor tightening around her middle and gradually, so slowly, suffocating her internal organs. Colour drained away from everything. Her mum's face dissolved into a pool of grey as she dabbed away tears with an already sodden handkerchief.

Hugging was never really done in their family, but Myrrh had to hold on to something. Robbie felt more like her family than the birth family she did not know. How mixed up it all was. People always liked to say blood was thicker than water, but what did that really mean? Did it mean you were the result of your genes, or did it mean you were always loyal to those with whom you shared a biological link? Myrrh liked to think it meant the opposite: blood was thicker and more complex. Water, on the other hand, was cleansing and pure; it could adapt and heal.

She sank in to her grief and layered it upon the seething mass of loss that was already there. Already fiercely guarded by her goblin as if it were a treasure, and he its keeper.

CAYENNE

Panic.

Panic.

This madness takes me and rapes me. I'm livid with rage, insane. Poised and alert I watch crustaceous creatures emerge from brackish pools, creeping towards me across broken land with gnashing claws and teeth. Their tongues protrude and retract as if to taste my scent and feed on my fear. I feel them snapping at my heels but can only look upwards to the moon's impartial face.

I lunge towards the oily slick of half-formed creatures. The claws of their pincers are jelly, unformed parts of my mind. The snarling teeth and crashing cymbals in my ears are mere percussion. If I sing the song of the moon she may set me free from this nightmare. I squeeze my eyes shut then open up my lungs and lift my voice to her, but the notes become a howling, primal scream.

I dare to peep through my half-open lids now blurred with tears and see my furrowed reflection in the dark mirror of the pool; here is a woman, not a she-wolf with sharpened teeth as I'm portrayed in my confusion. I see a face that is calm and serene for just a moment. Then the howling begins again.

Follicles burst through my once-soft skin, my bones stretch and break, and my tender flesh rips. The howling is louder, and I try to run but I'm bound by her rays, by her silky soft light.

I'm hypnotised. Even the grass beneath me conspires with her. She shows a face only lunatics and beasts of the underworld can fully appreciate.

The clouds shift. I sink to my haunches and howl from the depth of my new body. My shadow wolf brushes off creatures that are always there trailing me. The wind whips at my tail. I run.

They never take a concrete shape, those amorphous beasts from the pools behind me. I create them from the bile rising up my throat. They are mine; they are me.

From my belly I feel a distant, familiar ache. A sticky darkness oozes from my womb. It is warm and metallic, scented like hot flesh mixed with rust. I bleed but I do not die. I tear at the ground and wipe between my legs with clawed hands. With renewed vigour I leap into the pool of beasts.

As I rest on the bank between water and earth, I am aware of a movement but not before I smell his milky breath. I am dazzled by his pure white skin but choose to ignore the drop of fresh blood that drips from his bearded chin onto his moon-white tunic.

He smells like a mother's milk curdled with faeces. I want to touch him as he beckons to me with soft, open palms, but the fishy stench repels me. He opens his mouth and reaches, drawing out a black crayfish from deep within his throat; it is still alive and lashes about at the end of his arm as if he himself has grown vicious pincers. I recoil from him and he throws me a hurt look.

'Am I not your mother?' He drools with a blood-red grin.

A pulse of nausea washes over me as he tilts his head to one side, opens his mouth and reswallows the creature. I dry retch. I am next. I know it. He wants to swallow me whole too; he wants to consume my light and my darkness.

'You are not my mother,' I scream, lashing out with nails sharp as talons, slicing across his arms and legs, and ripping open his torso so that pallid liquid spurts from his wounds. Watery milk drains from his body and, deflated, he slumps to the ground like a greasy membrane. The once-enslaved crayfish scuttles free from his flaccid corpse back to the water's edge.

I cannot breathe. His beard wasn't dripping with *his* blood, but mine. I lick my fur; it tastes of fishy cream.

The membrane at the water's edge shifts into a memory. These cycles of hair, these cycles of skin. They will always die and be reborn. I am just passing through.

'I am going now,' I tell myself as the air fills my lungs again and the moon shows her waxy face.

Shivering with expectancy in my new skin I trust her. I feel what is right. I am no longer fighting the push and pull of her internal tides; I find rhythm and let my body enfold itself. The scars from my wild thrashings are no longer visible; were they imagined? I am not cut. I am pulsing with naked life. I am whole again.

The surging, swelling ocean has subsided. I allow the young blood of her new crescent to rise up my spine.

After the low growling of my throat is stilled, I hear music. There are no beasts in the waters beside me. The land stretches out beyond me, a silken shroud, where I sit newly born in this moonlit glade.

I have taken back what is mine, but the taste in my mouth is rank.

MARIAN

Holding it between her fingers, it looked like painted glass: blues, greens, spatterings of red. Marian had found the box of slides wedged in the corner with other unmarked boxes. She had meant to write on the lid but couldn't decide what to put. She still had a projector somewhere among her accumulated possessions. But she didn't need a projector to focus on the image. The slide she held in her hand was a scene she knew well. She had played it over and over again, after he was gone.

She had stood arm in arm with a man by the coast, watching the brackish water being whipped up by gusts of salty air, gulls dipping into the waves and toppling back with the air currents on angular wings. Along the shore a group of youngsters tossed pebbles from the beach into the foaming mass that crashed against the rocks. It was a moment filled with possibility, the great unknown. Transfixed for a time by the wild waters, she was unaware that he had moved along the cliff and was taking photographs of just her, alone, looking out to sea.

When she realised he was taking pictures she felt a rush of inhibition. She never liked to be centre of attention and certainly not the focus of one person's gaze. He returned to her side, and they slipped into each other's embrace. She remembered the anonymity of this. How much she liked it.

She didn't know, then, that they would create something together. In their connection they threw off sparks that would eventually set fire to the tinder lying at the edges of their lives. Tinder made up of human life and every action, every touch, built up to one big bonfire.

Another slide, the muted colours a close-up of their hands entwined. It made her shiver to remember his soft touch. He said he was fixated on her hands because it was the only part of her he felt permission to touch within the public boundaries of their relationship. She was still married in the eyes of the law. He was from another country, another culture.

His lips, always moist, always ready to emote some warped truth, as if he could not speak harm. She felt foolish now; how utterly romantic it all seemed. In hindsight, it was clear this man was never going to commit his life to a married woman who already had a child, a woman he had only met in passing. She had not even considered he would be moving on. She thought it was the start of something new.

She shivered to think of his hands on her skin. He couldn't keep them still when he spoke; his passion played out in gestures. They moved like wings of a great bird, and she was mesmerised by them. His hands, her hands, his lips, her body, her longing may as well be confined to sit in an unlabelled box gathering dust that he had probably long forgotten.

CAYENNE

I watch the lights above the lift doors flash from *1* to *3*, bile rising in my throat, my head spinning. When I open my eyes the lift doors open and I step inside, hand to my mouth, waiting for the slow descent to the ground floor.

I retch as the lift comes to a halt. I rush from the foyer and, just as I reach the street, I vomit at the kerbside, heaving up a tsunami of carrots. No one stops to ask me if I need assistance. Legs and feet scurry away from the pool of mess as I crouch over myself. They skirt around me, this staggering, muttering woman. Is that what they see? A mad woman? A fat drunkard? An old lush unable to hold her drink?

If I had the energy, I would lift my head and shout, 'I'm pregnant!' I could hold my belly, put on a show. I want someone to rub the small of my back and coo, 'There, there, dear.' For some kind stranger to guide me by the elbow to the nearest seat and sit with me while I regather myself.

If they thought I really was 'with child', would they offer me respect? Would they extend this to the other being I might be harbouring inside, not this fetid, festering mess of snakes that writhes in me, promising only pain and torture?

I blow my nose into my handkerchief and try to rid myself of the smell of the maternity ward. I was so close, but the nurses were all swarming about like bees, visitors were coming and going. But I saw one – a child – and I was so close, and I could have done it. I could have picked her up and walked right out. But the nurses. But but but.

Not the right time.

Too many eyes. I need to visit his stepdaughter at the mother-and-baby home, away from prying eyes and ears. Her time to birth is imminent. And that is when the answer slides so easily into my mind.

The one person I hate with all my being will provide me with the thing I want most.

All mine.

MYRRH

Myrrh traced her finger over the small nick that was below eye level on the painted-over wall. It was the size of a fingernail, as if scraped on purpose. She ran her finger over it again, making a mental note to fill it when she was doing odd jobs. Those annoying five-minute DIY tasks that mounted up without you noticing, but were too small to get out all the tools for unless you dedicated your entire afternoon to tinkering. That was what her dad used to do: hours spent in his shed tinkering, whatever that entailed. God knows why anyone would want to spend hours in a damp shed, but then again there were worse things to do, like morris dancing or jigsaw puzzles.

She'd have to sort out the wall before she got round to painting it, not that she'd ever decide on a colour. She wanted dark blue, 'Sapphire Salute'. 'Elephant's Breath' was old hat. She flicked through the colour charts without much enthusiasm. *Smoke and mirrors,* she thought. Wasn't it just something to fit a mood, and moods were always changing anyway. Who was she even kidding? She was decorating when she should be clearing out all the crap she'd accumulated over the years.

A corkscrew! That was what had made the mark. It must've been over five years since the place last saw a lick of paint. It had been over Christmas, sometime in between Christmas and New

Year. A get-together, booze, food, a buffet, bring a bottle or two. Even with the amount consumed that drizzly afternoon there were still full bottles left after the party. She had been waiting for a reply from her birth father, checking her phone at every available opportunity. It had begun to annoy her friends.

'He's probably just very busy,' she'd said. Then that loud friend of a friend piped up, 'Who's busy?' A haze of smudged lipstick, all red wine and garlic breath in her face.

'It's nothing,' Myrrh said, driving the corkscrew into the top of a bottle of white. She flicked back to her phone. Refresh. Nothing.

'You need to peel the foil off first.' The woman laughed. More lipstick. More garlic.

A glance at her phone. Refresh. Nothing.

'I know how to open a fucking bottle of wine,' she snapped back, and the hum of conversation in the room embarrassingly dipped.

attention seeker
little miss diva

Not now, she thought. *Not here*. But Goblin grew fat and powerful on her anger.

too busy for his little girl
he never wanted you
no one really wants to be around you
poor lickle orphan Annie
...or whatever your name is
bastard child

'Here, let me.' Someone reached forward to take the corkscrew, but Myrrh launched it across the room. God knows how it didn't take anyone's eye out. The sharp end must've hit the wall at an angle to make the mark, still visible as if a fingernail had gouged the plaster. She stared at it as if it were a portal to another world. Goblin had been stronger that night, with a rawness that sliced up her emotions. She went to the bathroom and locked the door.

As she sat on the toilet, she refreshed her phone at least fifty times. Still nothing.

didn't want you then
doesn't want you now

Maybe she shouldn't cover it up, or maybe it should be left as a reminder.

She'd cried after the guests had departed; she heard someone call her a moody cow; she'd thought they were all cunts for not noticing her distress.

This man, who had denied her from the very start, had only agreed to meet after she had contacted one of his sons, her half-brother, who had told his mum, and the slow unravelling of truth resulted in him finally having to respond. Too many people knew. There was no other way to get him to acknowledge her.

Perhaps we could do a DNA test, his denial still blatantly spelled out in his reply. *Just to make sure*. To be sure they were actually related, because names on pieces of paper could be errors. If that was what it took, she'd do it. She never cried: she was too upset to even speak about the ongoing denial. *'Dear Miss…'* He couldn't even spell out her name. He had no name for her.

She hoped she had ripped open their family with her intrusion. She hoped they were all bleeding out. Most of all, she hoped he felt the sting of her existence like the sharp prick of a needle extracting his cells. *'One does not miss what one never had…'* All these years and she wasn't asking for anything but the truth.

Goblin nearly choked on his own mirth.

truth will set you free
truth will bind you up in chains
truth will spin straw into gold

CAYENNE

I can't risk phoning my sister from the house, so when I'm heading home from visiting the girl I pull up in a sleepy village. I grab my purse from the car and enter the phone box. It reeks of piss and something worse. I try to prop the door open with my foot as I reach the receiver to check it works. A dial tone. Good.

The heavy door awkwardly pushes against my foot, so I let it swing shut and push the coins in the slot. I dial and wait. It only rings twice before she picks up.

'I can't believe it.' She sounds shocked, but I can sense the weakness still there after all these years.

'I know, me neither.' I grit my teeth bracing for the next lie.

'You know I miss you, sis,' I tell her. She likes when I call her sis. I'm her younger sibling, her only family. Maybe she still feels protective. Nothing changes.

'It's been too long,' she says. I make appropriate noises, tell her I've missed her so much. She's always been like putty. Maybe this could be the chance to reconcile our childhood differences. A new extended family. That's what I tell her.

'I just can't wait to see you again, Katherine.' She's the only one who calls me by that name. It grates on me to hear her say it.

I lay it on thick, add a little sob like its caught in my throat.

'Only if it's no trouble,' I add. Did she remember how we used to have to sit still in church? Me pinching her bare arm hard to make her squeal.

'When's it due?' she asks. We chat details. I can hear the yearning in her voice, that wheedling tone has never left her. Even when I used to force her to take the blame. The bruises blooming on her thighs from the beating I deserved.

'I'll need to discuss it with my husband,' she says.

Family stick together, don't they? Even when it hurts.

'I don't know who else to turn to.' As I speak, I know this is what my sister has been waiting for. The moment I tell her I need her.

The smell is ripe now. I'm not sure what it is, but it's filling up the phone box. I leave her question unanswered because she knows the answer. Always trying to do the right thing. That's my dopey sister. Maybe she got all the good bits, and I was left with the dregs.

'A baby in the family,' I hear her say, but I drop the receiver to look at the bottom of my shoe. I have trodden in dog mess, and it has worked into the ridges of my sole. I scrape my shoe on the edge of the window frame. It reeks.

When I pick the receiver back from its hanging cord, I hear the pips before it cuts us off. *A baby in the family.* Her last words. I scrape my shoe on the grass verge outside, back and forth, but even though it looks clean I know the mess is still there.

MYRRH

Unknown flashed up on her phone. Myrrh nearly didn't pick up, but something made her answer the call. She was just about to start the engine. Bags of shopping were in the boot, and it had started to rain.

'Is this Myrrh?' a woman's voice asked, calm but with an edge of worry.

'Who's calling?' Myrrh knew this wasn't a usual sales call. Her stomach flipped.

who's calling

who's calling

'You sent a message to my son.' The voice wavered a little. 'My name's Sandra.'

name me

name me

Myrrh felt sick. The rain pattered on the windscreen and made blurry patterns as she looked out at the other cars and people entering and departing the supermarket. Why did she pick up? This wasn't the right time.

not the right time

not the right baby

'I'm sure you have a lot of questions.' She was talking a lot now, 'I know we do.' A small choked laugh.

Myrrh was concentrating on one solitary raindrop making its way down the screen in front of her, its path mapped out, merging with the other droplets of water.

swallow it down
wallow
drown in it
choke on it

Why hadn't *he* phoned? They must have talked about it. Her, the son, the man who was named as her father.

spineless cunt
no-name baby
name me

'It's all come as a bit of a shock, really.' Sandra seemed to be doing all the talking when it was Myrrh who had all the questions. But they were stuck inside her, weighed down by Goblin.

'We'd like to invite you over, if you'd like?' An invitation, but now it was stated out in the open she wasn't sure at all whether she wanted to meet the man named on her birth certificate. Her stomach flipped and her mouth dried up.

'I'd like that,' she replied.

like that
like that

Goblin was ripping up her liver, chewing on her lungs. She thought the air in the car was going to evaporate. All the glass had steamed up, water streamed down the windscreen and the glass dripped inside and out. She was drowning inside her own car. After they had finished speaking, she stared at the phone like it was a loaded weapon in her hand. What had just happened? Someone she didn't know, another complete stranger, had made arrangements on their terms. And she had let them.

bad baby
hold out your begging bowl
lap up the spilled scraps

Myrrh wound the windows down and let the rain spatter into the car and splash on her arm. Anything to take away the twisted, gnawing in her guts. It was so huge she couldn't even breathe properly. This thing she held inside her seemed bigger than ever. Goblin was eating her alive.

CAYENNE

Anger. I used to like it when it was named wrath or vengeance. Anger is pure. Cleansing. Anger is like every emotion you've ever had all rolled into one big fiery beast. I think of my own father when I was growing up, his looming presence like a great black cloud towering over me. The only way I can manage these thoughts is to blast them with sharp spikes of lightning, piercing through the clouds until they are just pockets of mist floating away.

I have agreed to visit her while she is 'on holiday' by the coast. Her father is so shamed by the experience. He was not even aware that she was having sex. His little princess, defiled. Was she so naïve to think it wouldn't happen to her? Should I have offered some worldly advice when she was staying out late? No matter. The deed is done now. We have to get through this. He slams about the house, all fists and fury. I'm not sure I can face him while he directs all his anger at me.

She is wary of me, but I am the only link she has left with her father. I am the link to the baby. That is what I tell myself each time I gird my loins to meet her in that awful home for mothers and babies. It's nothing more than a halfway house for the unwanted. They know that. It shows on their tear-streaked faces awash with fear. Some look too young to even be left unsupervised, but God has somehow planted the fertile seed of another into their wombs.

I plant a kiss on her cheek before I leave and tell her it won't be long until things return to normal. If she only knew what was in store. She might not complain so much now.

MYRRH

They may as well have been talking in tongues. Family in-jokes were just another way of making her feel excluded, not part of the clan. She took a sip of the coffee, grainy and too hot, not the creamy way she liked. They were trying too hard to make her feel welcome, and she wanted them to stop. Suffocation as a tactic. Suffocate the intruder then get rid of her.

'Have another cookie.' Sandra picked up the plate and held it out at arm's length, as if feeding a zoo animal.

have another cookie
have another family
grind their bones
stuff them all down inside

She bit into it, but it felt dry and dusty on her tongue.

'Is there anything you'd like to ask?' Why was he letting his wife do all the talking? Why would he not look at her?

He was smaller than she imagined. They all were. She had blown them up in her mind to gigantic statuesque beings, towering over her with big hands and booming voices. She was a little disappointed that they were so ordinary. A bit like the family she had grown up with in more ways than she would like to confess, each with their own special scent.

'It was when Khufu was alive.' The eldest was flicking through his phone.

'No, it couldn't have been that long ago.' Sandra pushed the cookies around on the plate so they were evenly spaced.

'He was totally deaf.' The eldest looked up from his phone.

Myrrh had no clue what or who Khufu was. She glanced over at the man who was supposed to be her father, but he did not look her in the eye. Instead, he busied himself, straightening the tassels on the tablecloth, occasionally taking sips of his coffee, looking down or across at whoever was speaking, then dipping his eyes back to the tabletop.

stab him in the eye
make him look
make him bleed

'You said you liked art?' Sandra seemed keen to extract random pieces of information from Myrrh. Leading in with questions about what she liked, where she'd been, who she was.

'There's a very good exhibition on at the Tate. Have you been?'

who are you?
you are nobody

Myrrh could tell her husband was a proud man, no doubt used to getting his own way. An awkward silence penetrated a little too long, and she shuffled in her seat, remembering to breathe in and out. Her tendency to hold her breath was not a good habit.

hold it in
stuff it down
choke on it

'…Is that shift work?' Sandra still led the conversation and was now asking questions about Myrrh's job. They knew absolutely nothing about her. How she liked to twirl her hair around her finger when she read a book, how she sneezed when she woke up, how she hated sultanas.

All the questions Myrrh had harboured about who they were, what they were like, were redundant now. As they sat there together at that table, Myrrh realised that no amount of talking would make up for lost time. They were total strangers. His email flashed coldly in front of her like a paper cut slicing across her eyeballs. *One does not miss what one never had.* He had written that and pressed *Send*. He had been forced to write to her because she had blown apart his denial by contacting his son. Her half-brother.

He had used the word 'relation' unironically in his emails. *We met and went to the beach. This ended in a relation. We went to a party, I went back to hers, we had a relation.*

Relation. *What a stupid word to describe sex*, thought Myrrh. There was no relating involved. He had done his business and left her birth mother with the goods, a simple transaction. She could afford to be crass after all these years.

'Do you think we look alike?' Myrrh stared at her half-brothers' faces. Eyes, noses, mouths, chins. Was there a slight resemblance? They all stopped and looked at each other. Sandra sniffed back a laugh. She looked at her sons, at Myrrh, and then her husband, and then lifted her cup to her mouth.

'Maybe, our chins, like Dad's.' The elder brother laughed. She couldn't see it, not really.

Now here they all were, exchanging pleasantries, when all Myrrh wanted was some acknowledgement that he was her father, she was his daughter. Those offerings were not forthcoming among the teacups and tassels.

no one wants you
unchosen
unwanted
unwanted
unwanted

Maybe her goblin was right this time. Who was she to these

strangers, with their fancy framed photographs and vases of roses dotted about the polished surfaces of their home?

'Very nice to meet you, Miss.' He could not even bring himself to say her name, or had forgotten it already.

name me

NAME ME

Her blood was boiling in her chest, in her skull. She wanted to spit hot lava at his face. She wanted to stick her nails into his skin. She wanted his passive demeanour sliced apart with hot, sharp blades. Even then it would not be enough. It would never be enough to match the hurt in her veins.

She waited until she turned the corner before she let the tears spurt out and run down her cheeks in hot rivulets. *Fucking cunt*, she thought. Then she wound down her window and shouted it at full volume, not caring who heard her. Somewhere in the car, she heard Goblin choke on his smoky laughter.

One does not miss what one never had.

She could feel Goblin rise and rise and rise and then

GOBLIN

bite your tongue and fill your mouth with blood stuffitinstuffit
down choke on it you can't squash me down I'll always be here I
am meant to be here nothing nothing bleed WHO ARE YOU?
you are nobody a motherless loser *no one named you name me
name me NAME ME* your mother didn't want you damaged goods
who wants you who wants you who wants you? worm
in the dead mouth lost and found worms in the ground help me
help me find them WHO AM I? open the door trip trap
across the threshold *unbox the secrets dirty little secret* who do you
think you are? I can twist your guts so they shit out your mouth
your shitty words will spew out *you're the dirty little secret think
you know the truth, do you?* make it up make up the story hunger
will eat you up they leave the children in the forest dirty stinking
mothers fathers creep beneath the moon gleaming pebbles silver
pennies you will get nothing from me you will get nothing you
do not deserve breadcrumbs do you not know who you are? fool
leaving a breadcrumb trail seeking your own way home daddy
raises the axe the wind blows fall asleep in the darkest part of the
forest the dark night will eat you full moon rising

it bites

it stings

it burns

follow the breadcrumbs why are you heading back? What in the past can greet your heart the children must be saved the children must be taken save yourself a father knows best a mother knows best a father knows what scars he makes *lies all lies* want the fairytale want the happily ever after mummy daddy canyouhearme? never eat when you can feast on your own innards eat your tumours hold out your begging bowl little child fairest of them all grotesque hag fill your pockets with stones cross the bridge clip clop the windows are made of sugar nibble at my door said the witch I mean you no harm *mummy mummy where are you? what is my name?* too good to be true a forever family the gold is spun you cannot eat gold captured chained behind bars knock at the witch's door fetch me food feed me up I need more fat nothing but bones an empty seat at the table finger bones through bars kill it cook it chuck it out *baby* with the bathwater bad *baby* burn the *baby* burn the bridges clip clop trip trap blackened skin flames lick skin blistered raw show me how you howl at the moon miserably burnt dead hopes are dead set yourself free help yourself jewels in the ashes an open book an unfinished story swallow it down stories like rocks uncover beginnings once upon a time a motherless child sink it drown it burn it the stork carries the newborn like the wind found under a mulberry bush foundling I cannot see you in your belly mummy's tummy fairies in the garden open your eyes do you know yourself?

what is my name what is my name WHAT IS MY NAME?

name me gather round let me tell you a story a story about how you began meet Goblin confront your fears face the mirror reveal the secrets of the cave follow the breadcrumbs swallow the magic empty-handed free lost souls lost full of liars full of thieves hungry Goblin more give me more clip clop in the deep dark forest untamed unnamed cross the dark park discover a new story rewrite the tale *kill your babies* pack up the spinning wheel pick the strange pick the good ones fall to hell roam the earth like a goblin latch on spit up chewed remains puke it up pinhole beak long limbs insects for company droning on and on and on in your *headinyourheadinyourhead* fluffy bunny for the *baby* snout mouth dummy closed lips giftsforthe*baby* give me your bones rip out your ribcage examine her cunt for insects blackened charred remains trapped life inside pushed and extracted cut out punctured life a cockroach is your friend end of life wear your body outside itself ready for battle you look cute chopped up shredded on fire charred to ash burn your babies shit it out tickle tickle insect legs let's kiss with dirty snouts spades for the soil on your grave diamonds for lady luck hearts for myself clubs for bashing your head in hot dark lost wings eyes coming out of something WHO AM I? help! how many wings make a journey last a lifetime? too many noses, too many chins. hair trussed up for a ball bleeding lungs who breathes with a mouth open stink breath big lobed ears soil salt of the earth picked foetus a nut filled with promise start to push new roots from a split husk dark secrets

> *one does not miss*
> blank squish squish in your gut green bits slug on a tongue filled with liquid spilled on the grass drag it out blood drag it out blood
> *one does not miss*
> let me tell you a story you'll never believe it let me begin again Once upon a time upon a goblin…

MYRRH

There's tension in her stomach. He's taken the rope of her intestines and looped them into a bowline knot. Her eyes mist over but she keeps staring ahead, out at the endless road. He might ramp up his attention if she shows more discomfort than she's already feeling. She tries to swallow all the conversations but her mouth has dried up and her dry throat threatens a cough that may never cease. She reaches down for her water bottle and swigs a mouthful of tepid water, then another. A film of sweat coats her cheeks. It's a good job she is sitting down or her knees might buckle beneath her.

She can feel his eyes on her neck. Goblin. Zigzagging down the back of her head. He is close, closer than ever. Gaining strength minute by minute. She slows down for a pedestrian crossing. An old lady pushing a bag trolley in front of her. She could leap out the car, run, get away from the looming presence threatening to overtake her. But she crunches the gears and drives on. If she concentrates on the road, maybe he'll get bored and leave her alone. Maybe she could distract him. She starts humming a tuneless song. The dimples at the back of her elbows heat up, her hair starts to singe, his fingers slick down her head, slide around her throat.

Would anyone help if they saw her hair alight, flames licking the interior of the car, her face wide in terror? He's peeling back her skin now with his thoughts. The exposed parts snick against the fabric of her t-shirt. His words have become fat fingers, groping across the spaces she didn't invite him to touch. He wasn't invited. She feels like a toy. A captive mouse under a cat's claw. He's playing with her.

Outside the streets flash by, shop signs, doorways, people, trees, sky, pavements, houses, people, goblins, people, goblins, goblins, goblins. Her muscles tighten into dead meat. *This must be how an animal feels*, she thinks, *as they are herded to the slaughterhouse.* She is raw, cleaved apart and all because of him, because of this, because of Goblin.

The suburbs open up as she journeys toward home. She sees a child leap over a paddling pool, naked and free. But her skin is tarnished, and she feels the dirt layering over. A breeze – or his fetid breath – grazes her cheek. She'll stop the car. She'll find somewhere to pull over and stop and breathe. She'll regain her strength. Focus. Up ahead signs for a petrol station.

burn it
kill them all

CAYENNE

What if the man I live with is the ghost and my ghost lover is real? What if my real world is the world when I close my eyes at night? He puffs out his chest and can stand in a room looking important. He is fat. He is old. The hair on his head has thinned but his chin is bristly and coarse. When he nicks his chin, he uses a piece of toilet tissue to stick onto the bloody cut. He speaks with his mouth full of food; morsels get stuck round his mouth. He likes to wear dirty shirts and dirty trousers. His sink is full of feathers and his fridge full of blood. That ridiculous grunt when he finishes inside me. He is a liar. I hate him.

But he is mine, she is his and I have a plan now. I will get what I want. We will be a family.

My ghost lover is in my veins and lungs, and all the gaps that used to be me are filled with him. As I breathe in, I feel each contour of him enter me. As I breathe out I'm waiting for the next inhalation, hollowed out.

Last night he took my liver between his teeth, chewed on it with salty lips, and smiled up at me as I lay prone. It felt good to be eaten alive. He gnawed around my angry spleen, punctured my intestines and let the bile seep into my bloodstream.

'Soon,' he said. 'You will have it all, soon.'

When I woke my pupils were dilated and I puked until my tongue felt raw.

But I need him.

I'd let him do it all again.

MYRRH

All day frost had remained on the leaves, and when she looked out the window it was as if sunlight sparked like electricity where it hit the icy cobwebs. Nothing moved fast except the rooks and magpies, finches and tits all gathering food in before the temperature dipped again.

Myrrh slid a book off the shelf and as she opened it a small handwritten envelope fell at her feet. The cursive sweep of letters and the neat slope of the 'h' on her name stared up at her. She picked it up and slid one thin paper sheet from its envelope.

She didn't know anyone with the same name as hers. It wasn't even the first name she was given. She had assumed that her original name, Elizabeth, had been chosen in a hurry by a nurse or social worker just to fill in the gap in the paperwork. There seemed no record of Elizabeth anywhere in her paperwork relating to her birth parents. Perhaps it had been picked out of a book, or divined randomly. She doubted that it was because they had lingered, discussing how she, as a baby, looked just like an Elizabeth. Not a Liz or Lizzie, but Elizabeth. No middle name either. She was simply to be known as Elizabeth until the courts decided she could live with other parents, and it was up to them to decide on another name, a new identity.

Myrrh had once asked her mum how they had decided on her name. They had officially named her Katrina. 'We had a book of baby names,' she said. 'It's Irish, I think.' There was no Irish family connection, but the Celtic sound of it seemed exotic at the time. It just never seemed to fit. She would start a new school year and the register would be called. 'Katrina?' the teacher would shout out and Myrrh would put up her hand and say, 'That's me but it's not my name,' and the class would titter as she blushed into her hands.

Names chosen for her by other people were so off the mark she may as well have just called herself X. When she was in middle school she tried announcing to everyone, 'My name is *Katrina*.' But no one seemed to take any notice, and they all continued calling her Myrrh. It was totally fruitless to even resist the inevitable. Myrrh was the name that had found her, and she had to live with it.

Despite many years of explaining her convoluted name story to bureaucrats who eyed her warily when she said, 'My name *is* Myrrh, but it's not, if you know what I mean,' they didn't. Not even her sweet smile would make the blind bit of difference. She was beginning to feel like the fraud they made her out to be. She couldn't even call it a nickname. It was her name, the one she had grown into like her new identity when placed with new parents. In her passport a line had been added: *Holder also known as Myrrh.*

She re-opened the old envelope and began to read the spidery writing ...*you will have a better life... difficult circumstances... sorry...*

How often had this woman thought of her, this stranger who had given birth to her then relinquished her to a life she had no control over? That letter had shaken her. She had tucked it in a book to take with her while she was away on holiday. But it felt even more like she was grasping for something she would never have. The past was the past so she pushed those niggling thoughts to the back of her mind. Everyone had a past. Only she considered hers to be a large, looming shadow creeping up on her.

...sorry...

The only words she had ever received from her biological mother were restricted to just three sentences. Was she sorry? She sensed a slight reluctance or reticence to offer up information from that disruptive time, long ago. The address, the house in Cornwall that had seemed so empty, etched at the top of the page. Did she want to be found? She pocketed the letter and slid the book back onto the shelf. Outside the sun was beginning to break through the white air and unfreeze the landscape.

I'm not sure where to begin...

Myrrh scribbled down the beginning of her letter.

name me

My name is Myrrh...

my name is

You are named as my birth mother...

named as my

name me

Goblin gnawed away at her. He was not welcome. This was *her* letter. *Her* birth mother. What did he have to do with it?

what have you got to do with it

you're nobody

nobody wanted you

I have a letter from you...

you have a

you have nothing

I wanted to ask...

dead

dead and gone

What if she was dead? Myrrh put her pen down. She could be. People died. All that time had passed. She could be dead.

dead

you're dead to her

But she had to try. Myrrh picked the pen back up and finished the letter.

CAYENNE

A cowboy is singing about his broken heart. It is the woman's fault. She stole it and left him to die. Did she claim the fleshy muscle as her own, cut it out to keep, pickle it in a jar? Do you cut out the bad bits or the good bits? The bad bits are not so desirable so perhaps you cut out the good bits and what is left is all bad. Or do you leave behind the good, taking more care to extract the bad, focusing on what will be lost and forgotten? Either way, what is taken, or left, or discarded, will be forever changed.

This growing vitriol I have towards her is superseded by a dread that she holds all the cards. I have been visiting her now she has been 'sent away', but her father will not speak of her. Shame covers him like a shroud.

At night, my ghost lover whispers to me. 'Soon, soon, soon.' And I know that this is all part of the plan. That everything will turn out right and we will be a family. Sometimes when I lie in bed, I ask him, 'Why not me?' and he smiles and I know that it doesn't matter where the baby comes from. It is mine and mine alone.

Still though, I think back to my ghost lover and my head gets muddled with the dates but yes, months ago, he was there with me all the time as I lay my head on the pillow and closed my eyes. To think he has impregnated another, especially her, sickens me.

How can he be the father of her child, my child? He is the one pure and good thing in my life. But if he is, then I know with a certainty that makes the bile rise in my throat: that baby growing inside her is meant to be mine. My body is telling me that this time I will be a mother. Whatever it takes.

MARIAN

Marian put her notepad and pen down and went to fill the kettle. She would approach each stage of the pregnancy with magnanimity, a junction to be met and the direction decided at that point. She was certain of two things: one, she could not reverse the decision that had already been made for her. She was going to have the baby. Too far gone. Two, there was no way she could involve him. He had made it clear they were not *in a relationship*. They had never even been an item; they had never even reached the courting stage. He had referred to her once as a 'friend' and that was after they had slept together.

'There's nothing to get over,' he had said when they met for the last time. Easy for him to say when he was jauntily launching himself into a new life, in a new town, with new horizons that she would never witness. *His detachment would serve him well as a surgeon*, she thought.

She must have conceived the child after the party, end of October, Halloween. All those masks and costumes to hide behind. He'd already stopped working at the hospital, so it was a pleasant surprise when she glimpsed him buying drinks. She'd found him easy company and when he suggested he had nowhere to stay that night, so the simple solution was to offer him a bed. Her bed. It was the first and last time they were intimate but they both sensed something had been catastrophically altered. She could only describe it as a beloved object being stolen and, although returned later unscathed, it still harboured the scent of the thief.

A flicker of movement caught her eye. The postman on his rounds, whistling as he closed the gate and carried on down the lane.

Perhaps he didn't ever need to know. Now he had left the county it would be easy to keep this secret, but part of her wanted to name him. He was the only one she'd been with in years, and he was the father of the baby whether he liked it or not.

CAYENNE

Starlings cloud the grey sky. I notice the signs and say we need to take shelter in the nearby outhouse. We enter a large old stone building with no furniture; damp coats the walls. I make sure the doors are secure so we are safe from the storm. We find a gulley of water. Someone drinks from it and says we got lucky: the water is unpolluted. A cat skulks its way towards us, wary at first. It has escaped from whatever was persecuting it. It's wild, mangy and feral, wet through from a near-drowning, and looks as if it knows it has used up most of its nine lives.

I start the day haunted by a slight fuzzy headache that reaches up the side of my neck, and the tension feels as if I am all made of bone with no soft tissue. The feral cat from my dreams keeps reminding me of gushing water. I feel the need to be near the sea or a lake, but I'm trapped here with him.

We have said nothing for nearly thirty minutes. I clear the breakfast dishes and start to wash them in the sink. I want to remind him of those days when we first met. We talked and talked for hours. Now he has nothing to say, or nothing to share with me. I am invisible. I'm sure if I burst out crying, he'd just sit there, barely acknowledging me. Has the man no soul? I'm beginning to wonder. Since she has been gone he's been moping more and more, but it was his decision. For once I sided with her and said we could all stay here as a family and pretend the child was mine so her reputation would be saved. His fury won those violent screaming matches, and now she is near the coast ripening like a big, fat pear.

'Cup of tea?' I break the silence.

He replies, 'No thanks,' without even looking at me. I feel ice in his voice.

I strike up the conversation again. 'How is your head?'

'I've still got it but not so bad.'

'Do you hate me?'

'Not at all.'

'Do you love me?'

He nods.

I do not feel it.

'What does that love look like?'

'What?'

'What does it feel like?'

'It's hard to describe.'

To me it feels like a cold shower, a shiver, or metal grating against my skin until it's flayed, and I'm a shredded piece of meat.

I return to the bedroom and reach back behind my clothes in the wardrobe to where I have hidden a box in the wardrobe. At first I don't find it, and a sudden panic greets me, but then my fingers touch the edge and I pull it out. Beneath the lid are the things I have been gathering in readiness for my new life. I move the wooden mallet and rope to one side and smooth my palms over the soft nap of cloth, the tiny stitches so delicate on the baby suits and mittens. I have folded them and neatly placed them inside a shoebox at the bottom of the wardrobe. Each time I see a new item I purchase it and stow it away, ready for our time. This baby will want for nothing. I am praying for a girl. I feel it is a girl from the dreams I have been having. This child has been sent to me from my ghost lover.

'Soon,' he says. 'Soon.'

I am washed through with this life, but when the baby arrives it will be new and everything will be right again. A fresh start. All mine.

MARIAN

Marian felt a loneliness creep up on her. It had been draughty in wintertime, but the view of the sea chilled her more than the draught. All that endless water filled her with melancholy.

She would make herself eat but even fresh vegetables from her garden lacked flavour and appeal. She tried to conjure up a picture of the growing baby, ruddy faced, jolly round curves in almost all parts of her body, cheeks, arms, hips and calves, even the tops of her feet. A bouncy, healthy baby.

A part of her had flown away and tried to follow the baby, forever searching. Her colour seemed to fade from its original hue. She had always regarded herself as a mixture of rose madder and burnt umber, yet overnight she took on the cooler tones of a neutral grey.

The darkness had consumed her so much over the past months that, at first, she found it hard to benefit from the light of the hot summer season. As if the bruises on her heart were quite visible to everyone else.

Her son sought to apply his own unique kind of poultice in the form of random gifts. He picked her daisies from the lawn, gathered handfuls of stones still dusty with soil, and pressed them into her thigh if she didn't hold out her palm to accept them.

The guilt she felt about being *his* mother, yet giving her other child away to strangers, stung her most when she was alone. It

was her choice, she kept reminding herself. And time would heal.
Yes, time would heal. Time also churned away like a plough
uncovering forgotten items buried long ago under the earth.

CAYENNE

She is a fat balloon. She is a fucking melon on stalks. She waddles. But she is the host for my unborn child and I must wait for the perfect moment. Sometimes she fans herself, trying to disperse the overwhelming heat pressing against her body, and I wonder if the baby is cooking inside her, roasting in its own juices. She places her palms over her belly and rubs in wide circles. She catches me looking sometimes and wrinkles up her nose as if she smells something bad. It is time for me to go. I cannot be seen with her. Someone is bound to notice.

It needs to be a clean transition.

MARIAN

When she received the letter it wasn't as shocking as she expected. She read the words over and over, neatly written in black ink. The word 'mother' striking hard at the iron railings around her heart. She choked back a sob. All these years of not knowing how she was, where she was. Where had she been that day when the girl had visited unannounced? She rarely went far. Bad timing. A missed chance to connect in person.

She recalled a letter she wrote, years ago. The careful words she used.

She heard a continuous painful buzzing from the corner of the conservatory. A trapped bee struggling behind the low table and potted plant. She put down the letter she had read a thousand times or more and looked through the gap to see a spider tormenting the poor bumble bee almost twice its size. Part of her carried the mantra that you must never interfere with the natural course of events. But didn't that make her a hypocrite?

She could not leave it to die. It was trapped and no amount of buzzing could free it. Carefully she broke the cobweb with the end of a fly-swatter and scooped up the swaddled bee coated in dusty, sticky strands.

Carefully lifting the bee and its gruesome shroud, she took it outside and pressed the edge of the swatter to the trailing mass of dirty cobweb. The bee struggled on, its quest for survival admirable. She half expected to see a swarm appear to rescue it, carry it off like a Greek myth, summoned by its defiant death throes.

Finally, one of its transparent wings squeezed away from its trap although its back legs were still coated in dust. She didn't want to touch it, afraid of stinging herself. *The bee only stings when it is the last option. And that sting is fatal to the creature itself.*

Did she have a choice now? After all these years of not knowing where her daughter lived, what she was doing, or even what she had grown to look like, she was faced with a decision. She didn't have to meet her; the option was hers to decide, but a part of her already knew she would. Curiosity would sting her until she acted.

She looked again at the photograph enclosed with the letter, searching for resemblances, yet all she could see was his face staring back at her. He had even managed to claim the visual aspects of the child she had nurtured inside those lonely nine months before she was born.

CAYENNE

I mimic her as I have been doing, how she walks, how she sits. The phrases she uses when she is talking about her pregnancy. I've heard a baby can drain all the goodness from your body. These phantom symptoms are getting too much. My back aches as she tells me how her back aches.

My visits to her have become more frequent at the home. As her belly grows so, too, does my closeness to her. The child has forged a natural bond between us. I think she trusts I know what's best for her and the baby. She says *thank you* a lot. The feisty girl who used to throw me looks of disdain now greets me with a smile.

'We both want what's best,' I say to her and gently stroke her hand.

'Thank you,' she replies.

And all the while, at night, he comes to me and whispers, 'Soon.' And I know we will be happy.

I open all the windows to let the pathetic breeze waft through the office; then, as planned, I say I'm sick and need to go home. I guzzle down some sour milk I've kept in my bag for a few days. Then I vomit, making sure one of the nosy cows hears me retching in the cubicle.

MYRRH

Was she rescued or saved? Was she chosen by her parents or did she choose them? What were the terms of the contract? What was she to believe? There was a noticeable shift in others' demeanour when she said she was adopted.

She sensed a change in the atmosphere as if her predicament might be catching. Then all the questions that followed felt like a bombardment.

Who are they?
What do you know?
Will you look for your real parents?
Have you found them?
What does it feel like?

It was as if they had been presented with this vulnerable piece of information but had no idea how to handle it. A hot coal. A loaded weapon. An explosive to be disarmed with question after unanswerable question. It just seemed to fuel Goblin even more.

who do you think you are?
you know nothing
you're not real
you're not special
no one wanted you

But she *was* wanted. Wanted so dearly and so desperately by her adoptive parents. The paradox was catastrophic. She did not slip into the world alone to have others judge her for decisions made at her birth. She had already judged herself so harshly, grieved so deeply. She had been haunted by the goblin so long she didn't consider it was not her, never needed to be part of her.

no one will ever love you
you'll always fuck it up
always have
always will

Even now his whining voice was present. She had been the child left in a basket on river full of crocodiles; she had been delivered by a stork; she had been Rapunzel in a tower; the adored Tom Thumb; a fairy child switched at birth; she had been Jane Eyre, Oliver Twist, Heathcliff. She had forced herself into so many personas there was no way of knowing who she really was. And now this. Was it all a mistake? Should she have lived a completely different life with a different family?

'How did you decide to pick *me*?'

'We'd had lots of meetings. It wasn't an easy process,' her mum replied.

'But they told you some things, I mean, about me,' Myrrh could not look at her mum's face. It was hard enough to ask these questions without her mum witnessing her physical discomfort.

'Yes, we had a few pieces of information.' Her mum wrung her hands on the tea towel.

'Like what?' Myrrh would not let go, not now the subject had been broken open and was trickling out of the wound.

'We knew you were born in Cornwall. There were some difficulties with the paperwork.'

'What sort of difficulties?'

'The father wasn't playing ball.'

'What do you mean?'

'He said it wasn't him. Even though she had named him.'

'I found out who she was.' Myrrh couldn't say the word 'mother'. She was here with her mum. This other woman was not a mother to her. 'She was still at the same address.'

'You met her?' Her mum's voice changed. A sharp edge of hurt slipped like a knife into Myrrh's belly.

'I drove to her house.' She wanted to say, *she didn't answer, she didn't want to see me*. But she didn't.

'I met the man she said was my father, as well.' Myrrh couldn't stop now the secrets were being uncovered. 'He's married, with sons.'

'Oh,' was all her mum replied. 'I didn't know. We weren't told very much, like I said.'

'But you must've known it was me you were getting?'

'We were in a difficult position. We'd waited so long.'

'Mum?'

'There was another baby before we found you,' her mum blurted out.

look at what you've done
the mess you've made
blood all over the carpet

Myrrh sat down at the kitchen table and felt a lump grow fat and heavy in her throat. *Try and be sensitive, try and be sensitive,* her inner censor flashed its red beacon, but the words had to come out eventually.

'Another… You didn't really want me then?'

'Of course we *wanted* you.' Her mother turned from the sink and wiped her hands on a tea towel.

no they didn't
no one wanted you

'But what if that other couple hadn't changed their minds? I wouldn't be here now with you, would I? I wouldn't actually be your daughter.'

'But you are.'

not really
they didn't want you
'So I was the second choice.'
never a first choice
or any choice
you have no choice
'That's not what happened. You were meant to be our daughter. You *are* our daughter.'

Her mother sat down and wrung the tea towel between her hands.

'We were devastated when they told us the news, but we got you. We got *you*, Myrrh.'

'The names on my birth certificate… that's the truth?' A low growling started up in Myrrh's head, like the approach of a swarm of wasps.

'Yes, as far as we know. We weren't told very much about your circumstances other than your mother couldn't keep you because she had had an affair with a doctor and was living on her own. It was different back then.'

'Do you know what happened?'

Her mum swallowed and looked down at her hands again. 'We didn't want to tell you any of this. It wasn't very pleasant. They didn't tell us much, but we read about it in the papers and put two and two together.'

'It was in the papers?'

'When the woman went to trial. There had been problems in the family for a long time it seemed.

'It was horrific. All we got was a phone call saying there had been unfortunate complications with the birth. We knew straight away it was her. The girl in the paper.'

Myrrh looked at her mum's face wanting to ask more but smoke filled her vision.

name me

you took my life
murderer

Her eyes clouded over. She crashed to the floor and met darkness.

CAYENNE

As I approach, I see four, maybe five, birds on the road. A flash of blue and white gives them away: magpies. Not just five, more. Six, seven and they scatter to the trees lining the narrow lane. One for sorrow – I list the rhyme in my head – and seven for a secret never to be told.

Fresh remains of roadkill, fur and flesh ripped open by beaks and tyres, dotted with flies. The head of the young fox crushed so its eyes comically protrude. I know those birds are watching, waiting for me to pass so they can return to their feast.

Seven for a secret never to be told…

My ghost lover shows me the baby in my dreams. I see cells multiplying, tiny limbs grow fingers and toes. Little hairs atop their head begin to sprout. *Soon. Soon. Soon.*

Not long, my sweetheart, I whisper to the air and step over the mangled carcass of the dead fox. Leave it to roast in the hot midday sun.

MYRRH

you stole from me

A whining voice, grating against her insides.

they are mine

Something is pressing down on her chest.

love comes to you, but it is mine

This is bad, really bad.

they didn't want YOU

She can hear but it's so dark even with her eyes wide open.

give me back what is mine

She knows this voice.

you don't belong you don't belong you don't belong

She can hear something familiar. Running water? Maybe birdsong. The rapid thud of her heartbeat in her ears makes her want to sit up. But she is pinned down, swaddled.

give me back...

The voice pleads with her. She has never once answered it back. Why has she never answered it? Because she can't see it. There is no way she can see it in this darkness.

lies, all lies...

There is a scrape of wood like a chair leg on the floor. She thinks she can hear another's breath near her face but still she cannot move. The scrape of a cool fingernail on her cheek. A thought spirals toward her: could it be a knife?

not dead not dead

The voice is whimpering now. She opens her mouth and can hear herself draw in a breath. Goblin. It is Goblin. Always with her. 'Goblin?' she asks.

you took my place

'I was just a baby,' she says.

I was just a baby

'I was just a baby like you,' she says.

you took what was mine

stolen

you cut me out

burnt me up

She can feel the pressure easing from her chest. *Keep talking, keep talking*, she tells herself. 'We didn't have a choice in what happened to us.'

lies, all lies…

'It wasn't your fault,' she says. The feeling returns to her legs, her arms, a cool breeze wafts over her face. There is a flicker of light.

'Do you hear me? It wasn't your fault.' She chokes back tears, gasps for air. No longer pressed to the ground, she finds her body soften, and there is a familiar face in front of her.

murmur

murmur

myrrh-myrrh

myrrhmyrrh

myrrh

myrrh

But it is not the goblin's voice, it's her mum's. Her mum is kneeling over her, flapping a magazine to create waves of cool air. She is pressing a soft, moistened cloth against her brow and saying her name over and over as if it's a question.

'Myrrh? Myrrh?'

As she focuses, she sees her mum's face. The face that has always been there for her. Not a face resembling hers in physical features but with the familiarity and bonding that comes with time. The one who has cared for her all her life with a fierce protective love.

Her *real* mum, her *proper* mum.

CAYENNE

Her hands rub circles over her engorged belly. She sighs. Her shoulders are loose and her back arched. She is a grotesque human balloon.

'He needs you. He needs you there with him,' I say. 'He is at the hospital. We must leave right away. An accident.' Her eyes already filling with disbelief, then fear. Her heavy body lumping down into the car seat.

'My bag,' she says. 'My things.' But I press on with the urgency.

'There's no time,' I say. 'We must hurry!' We need to leave now, and she is in no fit state to drive. Time is running out for all of us. She questions me but has little energy to argue with my momentum as I bundle her into the car.

I drive like a maniac through the country lanes, relishing each twitch in her legs, each knuckle on her hands turned white. 'Please,' she says, 'please be careful.' How dare she question my care of the baby. She is just the host. The carrier.

My mind strays to what I must do. It has been filling my head as much as the baby is filling her body. We are both gestating something that will change us forever.

Her eyes glance up at the dual-carriageway signs as I swerve onto the slip road. I feel her glance across at me. *It's quicker this way*, I tell her, *trust me*. Trust me. Why should she trust me? I'm a monster, aren't I? But what else can I do? There's no turning back now.

MYRRH

'Every family has its secrets.' Her mum knelt by the flower borders with a trowel in hand. Myrrh had found her in the garden and now stood beside her, looking up and down at the neat rows of bedding plants her mum had already planted that morning, the pretty bright faces of the flowers turned upwards towards the sky.

'Why didn't you tell me?' When Myrrh needed an answer from someone or to resolve the whirring mass of uncertainty in the pit of her stomach, she stuffed it down until the need was satiated, until her goblin was fed. It felt like a heavy anchor wrapped around her middle. It felt like she'd never be rid of the weight of it and she'd drown waiting.

'It didn't seem important for you to know. It doesn't change anything, does it?'

A blackbird noisily chattered across the lawn and flew like a fast arrow up and over the garden fence out of sight.

Her mum speared her trowel into the earth, tipping the clod out next to the freshly dug hole. She upturned and tapped the base of a pot of petunias, and then gently inserted them into the ground.

'Would you still have adopted me?'

Her mum was silent for a few moments.

'We wanted you,' she said. 'You were meant to be ours.' Myrrh's mum sat back on her haunches and took off her gardening gloves, and then pushed her glasses back up her nose.

She stayed with her mum, just for a little while, and over the days Myrrh gleaned pieces of the story. The start of her life moulded back together, combined with all the other random elements, a kaleidoscope of colours merging and changing as her mum divulged what she knew, what her parents had been told.

'She'd made up a whole story, so when the baby was born she could pass it off as her own.' She thought about that girl and her poor baby. How someone's actions could impact so many other lives. 'Put the kettle on. We'll sit outside for a bit, shall we?'

A bee lazily buzzed from flower to flower gathering its nectar. Thoughts swarmed around Myrrh's head like a cloud of noisy insects.

'You know, I had a feeling that the baby wouldn't be ours.'

'Did they tell you what happened?'

'No. I suppose we found out like everyone else. It was all over the news back then. Such a horrific crime.'

'Did she think it was hers to keep?'

'Who knows what went through her mind.' Her mum took a gulp of tea and bit into a custard cream. 'We had no idea what was going on. All we were told initially was that our potential placement had changed. Then you came along.'

'My birth mother couldn't look after me?'

'It was too much for her on her own. You were due to be placed with another couple, but they backed out. Back then they hardly told us anything, but it didn't matter. You were meant to be ours.'

They had been told a few scant details, but most of the story came from the grubby tabloids that latched on to the facts like bait: a pregnant teenager, a brutal attack, a mugshot photo on the front page staring out without remorse, lank black hair and hollow eyes.

'What was the other baby called?' Myrrh couldn't picture such a tiny creature.

'I don't know,' her mum replied. 'I don't think the poor thing ever had a name.'

CAYENNE

'Why are we not heading to the hospital?' She scowls at me and squeezes her hand so hard on the door handle that her knuckles turn white.

'I need to get some things.' I carry on accelerating and pass the exit sign, hoping she calms down. I can't have her agitated. It's not good for the baby.

'But can't we just go there first?' She edges further in her seat.

'It won't take long.' I grit my teeth. What little patience I have is wearing thin with her questioning. Why won't she just shut up?

The windscreen is coated with dust from the dry ground. There's been no rain for weeks. I flick the wipers on, and they creak jaggedly across the dusty windscreen. She grimaces and cradles her belly with both hands, but I don't look over. I need to concentrate on where we're going.

'I don't feel well,' she says. 'Please just pull over.'

I see from the corner of my eye that she is arching her back and pushing her hips forward, hands cradling her girth. I need more time. She can't give birth in the car.

'Just a bit further,' I say as I turn off the main road into a narrow country lane. I pass a few gateways, praying that we don't meet anybody. The grass is high and swishes as the car passes.

'I need to lie down.' She looks over at me then back out the window, scanning the hedgerows, a film of sweat on her top lip.

Then she lunges at the steering wheel. I instinctively smack her hand away then squeeze my nails into her arm. The stupid, stupid bitch! I always thought I was stronger than her, but never underestimate a mother's raging hormonal strength. Hot tears spring from her eyes.

'You mad cow!' she screams, rubbing at her arm, but her words bounce off me. 'I never knew why Dad got involved with you.' She spits the words at me, but it means nothing now. 'Turn the car round. Take me back.' I scan the road and look behind in the mirror. There are fields around us so I pull up near a gate. Before I have even turned off the engine, she has swung open the car door and is heaving herself out.

'Wait.' I reach out to grab her but narrowly miss her arm.

In my mirror I watch her waddle back along the road. The bitch was lying. She is not going into labour. She has faked it: now it will be harder to get her where I want her. I launch myself out of the car, not even shutting my door, which hangs open like a gaping mouth.

'What are you doing?' I try and sound reasonable. 'We need to get to your father.' I catch up with her, but she pushes me away and carries on walking. I look back to the car, but even if I try to follow she might veer off down a track and I won't be able to find her.

'You're a crazy bitch!' she spits in my face. 'I don't know what my father ever saw in you.'

'That doesn't matter now,' I say, trying but losing any powers of persuasion I may have had. 'We need to go. We are just wasting time here.'

But she stomps onwards, so I have no option. I look behind me to check we are alone, then I crash into her full force with my shoulder. She loses her footing, stumbling hard on to her knees as she tries to break her fall. Her arms instinctively cradle her belly. She turns to check where I am then struggles to raise herself back to her feet.

'Keep away from me!' she hisses. I can tell from the look on her face that she knows I am not messing around anymore. I walk to towards her and grab her hair.

'You are coming with me,' I tell her. She scowls at me, but I see fear freezing her to the spot.

'Please, my baby.' Snot drips from her lip and her knees are grazed and blood-streaked from the fall.

'Your baby?' I sneer, and burst out laughing. 'Whatever made you think it was your baby?'

Her stupid face cannot comprehend what I am saying.

She tries to walk but her legs buckle under her, and she is back on all fours by the grass verge. I am wasting precious time with this annoying divergence when I realise this could be better than my plan. I walk back to the car and ignore her shouts behind me.

'You can't just leave me here,' she yells. But I walk back to the car and retrieve the bag I have wedged behind the seat. When I walk back to where I left her, I see her clambering over a stile at the edge of the field. She is making her way along a footpath through the trees. It doesn't take me long to catch up with her. She doesn't even have time to turn.

I bring the mallet down hard on her skull. Only one strike and she is out cold.

As she crumples to the ground, I know what I need to do. I upend the bag, but the knife is not there. There is no time to get back and search the car, so I use the sharp edge of the car key, sawing hard until I break the skin on her belly.

And it is quicker than I expect. Fluids spill onto the grass. There is no infant cry, but instead a sad grey creature, slimy and wet, as if formed from the deepest ocean, sits within. I cut it free and pull it out of her body, but it remains limp in my arms.

It looks like a tiny goblin, all screwed up and ugly as hell. It has arms and legs, but they are bony and scaled like a fish, its head is too large for its body.

The baby I have been yearning and praying and waiting for is a monster.

MYRRH

They sat side by side drinking tea on the garden bench by the back door. In the field opposite a few cows were grazing, rubbing up against the metal gate so it creaked like old bones. A pigeon landed in a clatter on the wooden fence. Myrrh took a sip of tea and tried to fully breathe out. The emotions seemed to be stuck in her chest like a hard, watery bubble waiting to burst.

Her mum swallowed and continued talking about the broken fence panel, how the willows would need trimming back this year, how the grass seemed to grow an inch overnight and needed cutting again. Myrrh let these practical observations ground her to the seat. This is what they'd always done, her mum and dad, to keep her rooted and safe.

Come on, do your worst, she thought, addressing the goblin, but it was silent for once.

CAYENNE

I hold the deformed creature in my arms, trying to understand why it looks this way. This is her/my baby. My newborn spawned by another, yet it has misshapen arms and legs. Its head is bigger than its body, its face long like a horse with bulbous eyes either side.

I throw it to the ground and scrabble away from it. I don't want this devil near me even if it had survived. All that waiting and my reward is a demon child.

I wipe my soiled hands in the grass and remove my shirt, which is smeared with blood and bodily fluids, but I cannot take my eyes off the mess in front of me. She is sprawled on her back, her dress rucked up above her waist to expose the jagged scar.

Then I realise that the creature is not dead. My eyes swim in and out of focus as I watch it try to sit up, its massive horse head wobbling from the weight on its tiny neck. Its legs are thin spindles, and thick hooves dig into the dirt. As it raises itself up, deformed arms unravel to form bat-like wings, thin sheets of skin webbed between the bones. I stare as it opens its mouth and spews out a stream of mucus. Tottering ungainly on its newfound legs, it stretches out the wings, and then it launches itself into the air.

I stand and watch as it zigzags a flight across the field, gaining height with each flap of the monstrous wings it has grown. Then, as if it has been shot down, it plummets to the ground. The creature fizzles and crackles like burnt meat on a skillet. I run toward it and retch as I smell its seared flesh.

It is not until I am blinded by blue lights flashing in my eyes that I realise I have been sitting here in the grass beside the tiny burnt goblin creature that should have been my child.

There is no point running now.

MYRRH

'What were they like?' Her mum cradled her mug with both hands. They both sat breathing, alive, side by side. She remembered someone explaining in an anatomy class, the lungs inflating like angel's wings. Myrrh looked at her mum's face, as she considered how to answer her. The bright striped colours of the earrings lay against her mum's neck: red, yellow, blue and green. She'd always brought colour in her own gentle way, subtle touches added without force, like a rainbow or a bunch of sweet peas.

This memory will resurface from time to time, years from now, when her mum has been laid to rest, those colourful earrings among items donated to a charity shop where a customer will see them on a glass shelf and think they remind her of happy sweets, so she will buy them to wear with her new red jumper, and her friends will comment how nice they look.

Myrrh tried to recall her trip to Cornwall, the house, the waves crashing on the rocks. The man who denied paternity, but was biologically her father, and his sons, and his wife. And. And. And.

'They were just someone else's family, I suppose.' How else could she describe these strangers who she had nothing in common with apart from genetics?

'It wasn't like on the TV shows, you know, where they reunite long-lost families.'

Her mum listened to her patiently. Patient. That was the word she'd use to sum up her mum's most admirable quality. Endless patience, eons of patience, mountains and miles of patience, eternal, unconditional patience and a real mother's love.

'You know you're my *real* mum, don't you? Nothing or nobody can replace you.' Myrrh felt the sting of tears in her nostrils and looked over at her mum, whose face wobbled a little as she reached inside her sleeve for a scrunched-up handkerchief to wipe her eyes beneath her glasses. Those eyes that had watched her grow up.

'I know,' she replied and patted Myrrh on her leg. 'And you are my daughter. Nothing will change that.'

Still nothing from Goblin. She felt nothing but a sweet tiredness behind her eyes.

'It's going to be a beautiful sunset again tonight,' her mum said. A breeze started up and the trees rustled like an appreciative audience. The sky was settling over the low horizon, peach and scarlet merging with vanilla, like the ice cream her grandparents used to dish up and coat with sickly strawberry sauce and hundreds and thousands.

'Will you tell Dad?' Myrrh could never talk to him about the important things, but he knew. Their weird, wonky love was strong. They were a family forged together by something stronger than blood and DNA. Fate had flung them together – mother, father, son, daughter – in a miraculous, messy, fateful union.

She had been born whole, like a seed containing unlimited potential, just waiting for the right conditions. She was not something damaged.

And now, after all this searching, she did have some answers but still could not convey exactly how it felt. After the heartache and tears, the bright rays of sunshine, of youthfulness, the flames of fear, there was always an unknown: a great green void in front of her like a vast expanse of undiscovered land, sea and sky. She would always belong to a continent of loss. But maybe now it could be viewed that way, with distance and composure.

EPILOGUE

A hot draught escaped from the loft hatch as the door was flung open to reveal a dark void in the ceiling. That dark hole was not just a shadow, but acres of memories that had been holed up in her subconscious. A cobwebbed inky blur of stagnant objects.

Myrrh climbed slowly to the top of the creaking metal ladder and peered over the lip of the hatch, half-expecting her unrealised dreams to grab her by the throat and pull her upwards into the attic. Instead, she saw the hazy outline of several boxes, rolls of carpet, a sad-looking artificial Christmas tree still clinging on to several glass baubles, and a large picture frame propped up on the rafters.

She trod carefully on the boards that had been laid earlier. It smelt musty, yet with the friendliness of an old forgotten coat. Tiptoeing over the boxes as if they were landmines, she banged her head on one of the rafters and swore.

She scanned the loft, not caring or even really noticing the large spiders that seemed to have grown out of proportion to their webs, and found her gaze settle on a horse's head. Its mane was coated in thick, sticky residue from years in an old attic, but she could see the faint markings of light and shade where it had been painted: a bay with ginger legs and a dappled back. She slid some boxes out of the way to take a closer look and pulled the wooden horse towards her. The horse shifted back and forth on its metal runners, silent and steady with a saintly expression. It was no more than half a metre tall, but as she touched it she felt her body shrink as she remembered gripping the crimson handles on either side of its head. She slid it towards the loft hatch and tried to lift it unsuccessfully over ancient, heavy boxes.

She remembered a part of her childhood. A good part. A time when she laughed as a child, feeling the free rush of a gentle breeze caress her cheeks, her mum's arm supporting her back as she held tight to that rocking horse with the cherry nose and handlebars as ruby red as Dorothy's slippers.

This time, she thought, *this time I'll close my eyes and wish for home.*

As she pushed the rocking horse further back into the loft space, she heard a soft thud. A cardboard box had been dislodged and spilled its contents of paperwork. *Hell*, she thought and hauled herself back up through the loft hatch. Hurriedly grabbing handfuls of papers and old photo albums, she started stuffing them back in the fallen box. She opened the thick plastic cover of a photo album and thumbed through the pictures of her mum and dad, some black and white. Faded faces smiled at her. Her dad in a suit and her mum with her arm slipped through his, her legs barely covered with a miniskirt and her hair piled up on her head. She had seen all these before, remarked how funny they looked, how young. 'We were young,' her mum had laughed. We were all young once.

A corner of newspaper was poking out the back of the photo album, so she turned the sticky plastic to reveal it. Parts of the text had transferred onto the hard plastic like an overhead projector slide. She carefully peeled the paper away, rough with age, and read the date. It was a cutting from the year she was born: *Heat Wave Splits Road in Two, Womb Raiders: Women Who Kill*. She scanned the article. Foetal abduction they called it. *Womb Raiders — women who steal babies.* She scanned the article: a woman, her unborn child brutally cut from the womb. Then, with a certainty that overwhelmed her, she finally understood. Goblin. A life unstarted. Stolen.

But she was always meant to be here. It was like a magic wand was waved around her so she would miraculously be placed with the perfect family. Perfect for all of them. The baby she had replaced had its own destiny.

She pocketed the sheet of old newspaper and crawled back out of the loft space.

END

ACKNOWLEDGEMENTS

This story has been festering inside me for a very long time. I wanted to write about obsession, loss, jealousy, choices, pain, hope. I wanted the main character to be adopted. Horror allows you to shine a light on the murky depths.

Huge gratitude to the team at Titan who welcomed me into the fold. Extra thanks to George Sandison for his enthusiasm, and Daniel Carpenter for his expert guidance in helping to shape this book.

For wisdom, encouragement, and endless support, I thank all readers, fellow writers, and the horror community.

Thanks to all my friends who accept my weirdness. I am lucky to have you in my life.

He probably can't read this but thanks to my darling, Vishnu, who keeps me company while I write and never jumps on the keyboard.

Most of all thank you to my family. I don't say it enough out loud, but I love you.

ABOUT THE AUTHOR

POLLY HALL is an award-winning author. Her debut novel, *The Taxidermist's Lover*, was a Finalist in the Bram Stoker Awards, featured in the *New York Times*, and won Gold at the IPPY Awards. Her memoir, *Blood and Blood*, was shortlisted for the Mslexia Memoir Prize.

Her writing has been published in anthologies and commissioned as part of interdisciplinary arts projects. She holds an MA in Creative Writing and teaches writing workshops. She lives near an old, haunted prison in Somerset, England with her cat, Vishnu.

THE BRIAR BOOK OF THE DEAD

A.G. Slatter

"This is an expertly woven tale of intrigue, magic, family, and righting old wrongs."
A.C. Wise

Ellie Briar is the first non-witch to be born into her family for generations. The Briar family of witches run the town of Silverton, caring for its inhabitants with their skills and magic. In the usual scheme of things, they would be burnt for their sorcery, but the church has given them dispensation in return for their protection of the borders of the Darklands, where the much-feared Leech Lords hold sway.

Ellie is being trained as a steward, administering for the town, and warding off the insistent interest of the church. When her grandmother dies suddenly, Ellie's cousin Audra rises to the position of Briar Witch, propelling Ellie into her new role. As she navigates fresh challenges, an unexpected new ability to see and speak to the dead leads her to uncover sinister family secrets, stories of burnings, lost grimoires and evil spells. Reeling from one revelation to the next, she seeks answers from the long dead and is forced to decide who to trust, as a devastating plot threatens to destroy everything the Briar witches have sacrificed so much to build.

Told in the award-winning author's trademark gorgeous, addictive prose, this is an intricately woven tale of a family of witches struggling against the bonds of past sins and persecution.

TITANBOOKS.COM

THIS SKIN WAS ONCE MINE

Eric LaRocca

Four devastating tales from a master of modern horror...

THIS SKIN WAS ONCE MINE

When her father dies under mysterious circumstances, Jillian Finch finds herself grieving the man she idolized while struggling to feel comfortable in the childhood home she was sent away from nearly twenty years ago by her venomous mother. Then Jillian discovers a dark secret in her family's past—a secret that will threaten to undo everything she has ever known to be true about her beloved father and, more importantly, herself. It's only natural to hurt the things we love the most...

SEEDLING

A young man's father calls him early in the morning to say that his mother has passed away. He arrives home to find his mother's body still in the house. Struggling to process what has happened he notices a small black wound appear on his wrist—the inside of the wound as black as onyx and as seemingly limitless as the cosmos. He is even more unsettled when he discovers his father is cursed with the same affliction. The young man becomes obsessed with his father's new wounds, exploring the boundless insides and tethering himself to the black threads that curl from inside his poor father...

ALL THE PARTS OF YOU THAT WON'T EASILY BURN

Enoch Leadbetter goes to buy a knife for his husband to use at a forthcoming dinner party. He encounters a strange shopkeeper who draws him into an intoxicating new obsession and sets him on a path towards mutilation and destruction...

PRICKLE

Two old men revive a cruel game with devastating consequences...

BLOOM

Delilah S. Dawson

"A literary pursuit for the ages."
Josh Malerman

Rosemary meets Ash at the farmers' market. Ash—precise, pretty, and practically perfect—sells bars of soap in delicate pastel colors, sprinkle-spackled cupcakes stacked on scalloped stands, beeswax candles, jelly jars of honey, and glossy green plants.

Ro has never felt this way about another woman; with Ash, she wants to be her and have her in equal measure. But as her obsession with Ash consumes her, she may find she's not the one doing the devouring…

Told in lush, delectable prose, this is a deliciously dark tale of passion taking an unsavory turn…

SMALL TOWN HORROR

Ronald Malfi

Maybe this is a ghost story…

Andrew Larimer has left his past behind. Rising up the ranks in a New York law firm, and with a heavily pregnant wife, he is settling into a new life far from Kingsport, the town in which he grew up. But when he receives a late-night phone call from an old friend, he has no choice but to return home.

Coming home means returning to his late father's house, which has seen better days. It means lying to his wife. But it also means reuniting with his friends: Eric, now the town's sheriff; Dale, a real-estate mogul living in the shadow of a failed career; his childhood sweetheart Tig who never could escape town; and poor Meach, whose ravings about a curse upon the group have driven him to drugs and alcohol.

Together, the five friends will have to confront the memories—and the horror—of a night, years ago, that changed everything for them.

Because Andrew and his friends have a secret. A thing they have kept to themselves for twenty years. Something no one else should know. But the past is not dead, and Kingsport is a town with secrets of its own.

One dark secret…

One small-town horror…

JUNE 2024

For more fantastic fiction, author events,
exclusive excerpts, competitions, limited editions and more

VISIT OUR WEBSITE
titanbooks.com

LIKE US ON FACEBOOK
facebook.com/titanbooks

FOLLOW US ON TWITTER AND INSTAGRAM
@TitanBooks

EMAIL US
readerfeedback@titanemail.com